SECRETS BETWEEN THEM
C.J. Carmichael

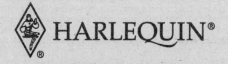

TORONTO • NEW YORK • LONDON
AMSTERDAM • PARIS • SYDNEY • HAMBURG
STOCKHOLM • ATHENS • TOKYO • MILAN • MADRID
PRAGUE • WARSAW • BUDAPEST • AUCKLAND

ISBN-13: 978-0-373-78119-5
ISBN-10:   0-373-79119-9

SECRETS BETWEEN THEM

The Forget-Me-Not Friends

Harrison Kincaid   During his childhood Harrison and
                     his sister, Nessa, spent all of July and
                     August on Summer Island with their
                     parents. In his thirties, Harrison
                     married Simone and became the CEO
                     of his family-owned communications
                     business based out of Seattle.

Aidan Wythe   Raised by his mother in Seattle,
                     Aidan has been Harrison's best
                     friend for as long as he can remember.
                     They went to Yale together and
                     Aidan is Harrison's right-hand man
                     at Kincaid Communications.

Emerson Cotley   A local on Summer Island, Emerson
                     took over the family landscaping
                     business after his parents were killed
                     in a car accident.

Jennifer March   Her family owns the Lavender Farm
                     Bed and Breakfast on Summer Island.
                     She and Simone were best girlfriends.

Gabe Brooke   Gabe owns a real estate business on
                     Summer Island, as well as the local
                     newspaper. He married Harrison's
                     sister, Nessa, after Harrison married
                     Simone.

Simone DeRosier   Renowned jazz singer and pianist,
                     Simone started spending her holidays
                     with her father on Summer Island
                     when she was fourteen years old. She
                     coined the phrase "Forget-Me-Not
                     Friend" in her first Grammy Award–
                     winning hit.

Dear Reader,

Thank you for returning for the final story on Summer Island, a locale I first introduced this June, in the Signature Select Saga novel, *You Made Me Love You*.

In this story we see what happens to the last two of the forget-me-not friends—Jennifer March and Gabe Brooke. Jennifer, the loyal best friend, and Gabe, the spurned lover, have both been marked by the death of their friend, famous jazz singer Simone DeRosier. Finally it is time for them to deal with the past and find their own happily-ever-after.

The inspiration for the bed-and-breakfast where most of this story takes place came from a lavender farm I visited in Kelowna, British Columbia, with my stepmom Gwen and daughter Tessa. It was amazing to see acres of lavender growing on the hills above Okanagan Lake. All I needed to do to fit this place into my story was to replace the lake with the Pacific Ocean and to add a sheep farm on the eastern boundary. And there it was...Lavender Farm Bed and Breakfast.

I hope you enjoy returning to Summer Island this one last time. If you would like to write or send e-mail, I would be delighted to hear from you through my Web site at www.cjcarmichael.com. Or send mail to the following Canadian address: #1754 - 246 Stewart Green S.W., Calgary, Alberta, T3H 3C8 Canada.

Sincerely,

C.J. Carmichael

ABOUT THE AUTHOR

Former chartered accountant turned fiction author C.J. Carmichael has published twenty novels with Harlequin Books. Highlights include a RITA® Award nomination for her Harlequin Superromance novel, *The Fourth Child* (which was also a *Romantic Times BOOKclub* Top Pick); a romantic-suspense career achievement nomination from *Romantic Times BOOKclub;* and a nomination for her Harlequin Intrigue title, *Same Place, Same Time* as a *Romantic Times BOOKclub* Reviewers' Choice Best Harlequin Intrigue of 2000.

C.J. lives in Calgary, Alberta, with two teenage daughters, and a dog and a cat. Please visit her at www.cjcarmichael.com.

Books by by C.J. Carmichael

For my daughter Tess and stepmom Gwen,
in memory of a lovely summer afternoon.

CHAPTER ONE

LEANING AGAINST THE FERRY railing, Nick Lancaster squinted at the horizon and wondered if the faint outline of land ahead was Summer Island. His adrenaline surged, making him as lighthearted as a kid at Christmas.

Almost there.

Finally.

If the island weren't so bloody remote, he would have been there sooner. But it had taken him more than a week to drive from New York City across the country, then over the border to Vancouver. Of course, he could have flown, but he hated flying and besides, he liked having his own vehicle. He'd bought his Land Rover with the royalties from his first book and there was an attachment there that amused his friends and family to no end.

Once in Vancouver, he'd caught the ferry and began the forty-minute crossing to his final destination—the vacation home of deceased jazz singer Simone DeRosier.

By now Nick knew almost everything there was to know about the musician: her early childhood in Hartford, Connecticut, her distant relationship with her professor father, her marriage to communication magnate Harrison Kincaid and all the details of her fabulously successful career.

Then there was her death. It had been reported as a suicide initially and that was what had initially attracted him to her story.

Why would a world-famous star with a doting husband and a young daughter take her own life?

Turned out she hadn't. She'd been killed. And with that turn of events, he'd been hooked. For the past twelve months he'd devoted himself to this project. Still there were unanswered questions.

Summer Island had to be the key. Simone had spent her vacations here, from when she was a teenager until the day of her death, three years ago. She'd met her best friends on Summer Island, the so-called forget-me-not friends she'd immortalized in her Grammy-winning song of the same name. Including Simone there'd been six of them at the beginning.

Now only four were still alive, and three of the four lived on the island. Nick intended to talk to them all, but one in particular had captured his interest.

The outside world didn't know much about Jennifer March. Somehow her friendship with the big star had escaped the media scrutiny of the others.

Nick had first gotten wind of her in an old article in *Vanity Fair.* Simone had mentioned a friend, Jennifer, whom she loved like a sister. Later, he'd found a photograph taken after one of Simone's New York City concerts. The star had her arm around a pretty blond woman. Usually Simone was photographed with men, so this was a real aberration.

The blonde hadn't been identified in the accompanying article, but Nick's curiosity had been roused as soon as he'd seen it. Could this be the Jennifer he'd been looking for?

It turned out his hunch had been right and his subsequent research had led him straight to Summer Island. He'd had a break when he discovered that Jennifer's family owned a bed-and-breakfast on the island. It had seemed like the perfect omen.

He'd asked his agent to book him a room at Lavender Farm for the month of September. Michele, of course, had been only too happy to oblige. She was as excited about this book as he was.

The little blob on the horizon was bigger now. Nick looked around the deck and noticed a man standing a few yards to his left. "Excuse me. Is that Summer Island?"

"Sure is."

"That's what I thought," Nick said. "Thanks."

He started to head below deck and as he passed by, the other man smiled. "I hope you enjoy your visit. Summer Island is a pretty special place."

"Yeah," Nick replied. "So I've heard."

There was something familiar about the man, but by the time Nick had gone to the washroom, then ordered a coffee, he'd forgotten all about him.

AFTER THE FERRY DOCKED, Nick drove his Rover from the parking level, down the ramp and onto the main road. He stopped at a big sign. To the right lay the north end of the island where his bed-and-breakfast was. To the left was the island's only town, Cedarbrae.

Deciding he was hungry and needed a meal, Nick turned left.

Summer Island was a place of rocky shorelines and thick rain forests. Even in town the trees were massive. Mostly cedars, Nick guessed, though he knew from his research that some of these were also Douglas fir and oak. Occasionally he spotted the twisted shape and smooth red bark of the distinctive arbutus tree.

He felt a long way from New York City as he drove along the deserted road. He wondered how a person could live full-time in a place like this. So small and rural and isolated. He had nothing against the great outdoors. But he'd only been here a short while and already it felt as if his thoughts were echoing around in his head.

He needed people.

A sign pointed left and he turned again. Here was the town and it was small. Most of the amenities were on the main street, which ran parallel to the ocean.

In less than a minute he'd seen the whole place. He circled back to Derby's Diner, a white clapboard structure, with green-and-white awnings shading the windows. The almost-full parking lot seemed testament to a decent lunchtime menu, so Nick nosed his Rover into one of the few empty spaces and went inside.

Only two tables and one booth were available. He was headed for the smaller table, when he noticed a redhead across the room. He did a doubletake, at first disbelieving, then amazed, then intrigued.

Molly Springfield was on Summer Island?

And then he realized he shouldn't be surprised. It seemed that everywhere he went in his journey to learn about Simone DeRosier, Molly Springfield had been there first. He still didn't know who she was, exactly, or what she wanted. But clearly it was time he made a more concentrated effort to find out.

He checked out her luncheon companion, a tall, thin blond woman, older, probably in her late thirties like him. He experienced a second shock as he realized he was looking at Jennifer March.

From the photograph he'd seen, he'd known Jennifer was pretty. But in person, she had a wholesome, natural beauty that was totally disarming. He could picture her in a shampoo commercial with a garland on her head and a meadow of wildflowers at her feet.

Wow, where had that image come from? Teenaged memories of flipping through his mother's magazines hoping to spot a lingerie advertisement?

The fact that Jennifer was seated with Molly Springfield was an interesting development.

The first time he'd run into Molly he'd tried to question her. But as soon as she heard that he wanted to write Simone DeRosier's biography, she'd gone running. She hadn't let him get near her since.

At one point he'd speculated that she might be writing a book, too. But if so, it would be her first. She had no publishing history.

It couldn't be coincidence that she was on Summer Island, though. And chatting up one of the original forget-me-not friends. They sure did look cozy, like they'd been pals for a while.

Both were dressed in yoga pants and colorful, formfitting tank tops. Their hair was tied back from pink-tinged cheeks. All evidence pointed to the likelihood that they'd just come from an exercise class.

They were so engaged in their conversation, they didn't even notice him. Quickly Nick changed course, bypassing the table and choosing instead the booth directly behind Molly. She couldn't see him here unless she turned completely around in her seat. Even then, she'd only make out the back of his head.

He picked up a menu and pretended to read it while he focused on their conversation. At first the words were just a blur. He closed his eyes. Concentrated.

They were talking about Jennifer's mother…

"HOW OLD WERE YOU WHEN SHE died?" Molly asked.

"Eighteen." The older Jennifer got, the more she realized how lucky she'd been to have such a happy, protected childhood.

Good parents, close friends, a storybook life in the storybook setting of Summer Island.

All that had ended after her mother died though.

"It's scary how fast your life can change."

"I know," Molly commiserated. She'd lost her mother a few years ago, too, which was why Jennifer felt comfortable confiding in her.

"I'm not sure how I would have coped without my friends. They were all amazing. Harrison helped me deal with the lawyers and the financial mess left behind because Mom didn't have a will."

"He's a rock, Harrison," Molly agreed.

"Gabe took charge of the funeral arrangements and wrote the obituary for the *Summer Chronicle,* while Emerson arranged for his family landscaping business to handle all the gardening and yard work at the B and B for an entire month."

"They really rallied around you."

"Dad and I were such a mess. We

needed the help. Aidan stepped in and canceled reservations and refunded deposits for the next few weeks so we had a chance to catch our breath. He even set us up on a computer system."

"What about Simone?"

Just the name brought a smile to Jennifer's face. "She was the one who made me laugh and helped me believe that the future wasn't as bleak as it seemed right then."

"She was something, huh? So famous and yet she still made time for her old friends. I wish I could have met her."

Jennifer said nothing to that. She wasn't so sure Molly and Simone would have gotten along. Simone never had trouble making friends with men, but women were something else. Not many could put up with being in the other woman's shadow all the time. But Jennifer hadn't minded. The fun of having Simone as a friend had been worth it.

But she couldn't see Molly willingly taking the backseat to anyone...even a

world-famous musician. Molly was flam-
boyant and confident in a way that
Jennifer envied.

"What about you, Molly? You must still
really miss your mom." She'd moved here
to make a fresh start after her mother's
death. Unlike Jennifer, Molly didn't have
any other family.

"Oh, I'm coping."

Typical of Molly to keep her answer
vague. Molly didn't like to talk about the
past. She was all about the future, or so she
said.

"Well I'm really glad you ended up on
Summer Island. I haven't had a good
heart-to-heart talk like this in ages."

"We need to go out more often. Have I
ever told you that you work too hard?"

"Only a hundred times." Jennifer
laughed. "But we can't all be free spirits
like you."

"Is that really how you see me?"

"Well, sure. You moved across the
country to an island where you didn't
know anyone and started your own yoga

studio. You're artistic and spontaneous, full of energy and brave…" Jennifer sighed. Not one of those adjectives could be applied to her. "In fact, sometimes you remind me a lot of Simone."

"You still miss her, don't you?"

"My aunt says too much. She says I lived vicariously through Simone and that it's time I learned to have my own adventures." Jennifer shook her head. "Can you imagine?"

Molly looked at her speculatively. "Actually, your aunt might have a point there."

"I don't think so." Molly, who had no responsibilities to anyone other than herself couldn't understand. Jennifer barely had time for yoga two times a week, let alone adventure.

"Frankly, I think we both could use a dash of excitement. Preferably of the romantic sort."

"Oh, really? Seen anyone who interested you lately?"

"Well…to be honest…" Molly drummed

her fingers on the table. "What about that friend of yours, Gabe Brooke. He's single again. I know he's rich and he's certainly gorgeous."

"Yes, Gabe is all those things. You should go out with him, Moll. Want me to fix you up?"

"What about you? You've known him longer."

"Yeah, but we've been friends forever. Dating would be weird." And it would. Though once she hadn't felt that way. "Besides, I'm good friends with his ex-wife."

"What happened there? Why did they split up? People say it was because of Simone but she's been dead for three years now."

"It's complicated." Jennifer rubbed her forehead. She didn't want to talk about it, but if Molly really was interested in Gabe, then she probably should know the basic facts.

"Gabe was in love with Simone for years, but when she married Harrison, he turned to Nessa. Nessa had always been crazy about him and she thought she could make their marriage work. But Gabe never seemed to get over Simone. He was always at her beck and call."

"Did they have an affair?"

"I don't think so. But Nessa felt emotionally abandoned anyway. And who could blame her."

Molly leaned back, wrinkled her nose. "He doesn't come out sounding like a very nice guy."

"Oh, but he is. You have to realize the power Simone had over people, men in particular. Once Gabe realized how much he'd hurt Nessa, he felt badly and tried to make amends. But it was too late."

Jennifer could sympathize with how Nessa must have felt. Once, Jennifer, too, had had a crush on Gabe. Years had gone by before she'd worked up the nerve to tell him. Only, just as she started talking, he'd blurted out how devastated he was that Simone was dating Harrison instead of him.

She'd realized then that Gabe saw her

as nothing more than a buddy, a pal, another one of the gang.

She'd told herself that it was just as well.

But now, briefly, she felt the burn of that old rejection. No sense blaming Simone, though. She couldn't help that all the men loved her. That was simply the way it had always been.

CHAPTER TWO

AFTERNOON AT THE bed-and-breakfast was Jennifer's favorite time of day. Her father usually took a nap on his reclining chair in the sitting room, with his sister Annie in the chair next to him, reading. This was when Jennifer was free to putter in her gardens and work on the lavender products she sold at a craft store on Saltspring Island.

Jennifer took her shears and a large shallow wicker basket out to the gardens in the front yard. She was expecting a new guest and this way she wouldn't miss her arrival. At any rate, the *Lavandula multifida* needed to be harvested again.

Her mother had planted the original lavender, for which the B and B was named. As the years went by, she'd started experimenting with other cultivars. Now there were lavender beds on all sides of the house, sometimes three or four in a row, with neat gravel paths between them.

The best time to snip the lavender stalks, if you wanted to dry them, was just when the flowers started to bloom. Jennifer stooped next to a perfect specimen. All around her bees were busy pollinating, but they didn't bother her as she carefully snipped at the stalks, just above the bushy plant growth.

Later, she'd tie them in tiny bundles with rattan and use them to decorate the jars of lavender jelly and vinegar she'd make during the colder winter months.

A peaceful half hour passed. Just Jennifer, the lavender, a few dragonflies and the bumblebees. Her basket was almost full when she heard a vehicle approach. She straightened, put a hand to her lower back and stretched. That must be Nic Lancaster, from New York City.

They didn't often have guests from so

far away. She was a little excited to meet this woman. Jennifer shaded her eyes against the afternoon sun so she could watch as a dusty old SUV came into view.

The driver pulled up to the house, then stepped out from behind the wheel. She frowned. Squinted. No, she wasn't seeing things. Her guest wasn't a woman, but a man. And while his vehicle looked weathered and battered, he definitely did not.

Late thirties, she guessed. Fit and naturally athletic judging by those shoulders and muscular legs. He wore typical summer outdoor gear—hiking shorts and boots, with a navy shirt, sleeves rolled to the elbows.

He'd been facing the house, perhaps reading the sign for the bed-and-breakfast, but then he turned and stared at her. Though about twenty feet of flower garden separated them, Jennifer felt a power in his eyes that made her mouth dry.

Their guests here were usually families, retired couples, college kids on break. She couldn't remember the last time a single man, an *attractive* single man, had checked in.

Which he might not do if she didn't stop gawking at him.

In her defense, she didn't think she was the only one having a moment here. The man in front of her seemed just as transfixed by her as she was by him.

He watched her approach with such intensity that she should have felt self-conscious. But, she didn't.

"Hi, I'm Jennifer March. Welcome to Lavender Farm." She put the basket on the ground, then held out her hand, amazed that she could sound so poised when she felt anything but.

"Jennifer." His hand was warm, his grip firm.

She removed a strand of hair the wind had blown across her cheek. "You're Nick Lancaster?"

"Yes. Sorry, I should have identified myself right away." His smile was a little crooked, a quirk that added a dash of self-deprecation to his confident air.

"Your reservation was made by a woman. I didn't know she was booking for someone else."

"That would have been my agent. She took care of the travel arrangements. I must say, I had no idea it was going to be so pretty here."

He looked right at her as he said that and her usual shyness suddenly kicked in. Was he flirting, or just being friendly? If he *was* flirting, what should she say in response?

Though Simone had been gone three years, Jennifer knew exactly what she would be saying if she were here. *Go for it, Jenn! Here's your big chance. Let him know you're interested and available.*

But now that it was happening, or *might* be happening, she felt awkward and tongue-tied.

"Um…why do you have an agent?" He was certainly good looking enough to be an actor. But he was also in incredible shape, so maybe he was a professional athlete.

His laugh was easy, natural. "I'm a writer. Michele Ashburn, the woman you spoke to on the phone, is my literary agent."

She never would have guessed that. He didn't look like the scholarly sort. "What do you write?"

For the first time since he'd arrived, he glanced away from her and hesitated with his answer.

"I'm writing a book," Nick said, finally.

"Oh." They'd had a couple of authors stay at the B and B over the years. One had been working on a travel guide for kayakers in the Gulf Islands, another had been doing an environmental survey for his doctorial thesis. "What's your book a—"

She didn't have a chance to finish her question as the front door opened and her father stepped out to the porch.

"It's time for afternoon tea, Jenn. Should I put the kettle on?" He paused at the sight of Nick, several yards away. "Is that our guest from New York City?"

Jennifer dashed up the stairs to hand her father his walking stick. He hated the cane, but she lived in fear that he would one day fall and break a leg. Since his stroke, he'd been a little wobbly on his feet.

But no damage had been done to his acuity. Even though her father could no longer handle the day-to-day work of running the bed-and-breakfast, he still managed the accounting side of things. He also checked the bookings every morning and made a point of greeting new arrivals personally.

"Dad, this is Nick Lancaster. Nick, my father, Phil. He and my mother started this bed-and-breakfast almost forty years ago."

Nick stepped forward to shake her father's hand. "This is a really beautiful place." His eyes were on Jennifer again, and once more she felt as if his compliment for the place included her.

Aunt Annie appeared from the side of the house. Though she ate her meals with the family, she slept in a small cottage on the property that had once been a potting shed. It was fully winterized now, with plumbing and a small kitchen.

"The toilet is leaking again," Annie said, before noticing the new guest in their midst. "My, my, who is this handsome fellow?" Annie approached Nick with her head tilted back, so she could see out of the bottom half of her bifocals. "Are you a friend of Jennifer's?"

"He's our guest from New York," Jennifer's father explained. "Nick, this is my sister. She used to work as a midwife in Northern B.C. but now she lives with us."

"A midwife. You must have many interesting stories."

Annie beamed, then in a move more fitting of a southern belle than a northern midwife, took his arm. "I most certainly do. You must join us for afternoon tea."

Jennifer was all but pushed to the side as her father and aunt claimed the new guest and led him inside.

So much for that romantic moment they'd been having.

Her chance for adventure was over before it had really started.

JENNIFER FOLLOWED THE TRIO inside, trying to see the humor in the situation. Wasn't it just typical of her life that the first time in ages she met a man who made her heart beat faster, her aunt had to show up on the scene complaining of a broken toilet?

Still, it would have been nice if she could have had a few more moments alone with Nick Lancaster...

"Nice picture." Nick paused to admire a painting Simone had given Jennifer for her thirtieth birthday. It was an Emily Carr, small, but original.

"Thanks," Jennifer said. "There's a story—"

"Tea, Jennifer?" her father reminded her. "We shouldn't keep our guest waiting. I can show him to his room while you put out the spread. He has the suite over the garage, right?"

"Dad," Jennifer said quietly. "The stairs?" He could only manage them with difficulty now and she knew it would be painful for him.

His face fell and she put a hand to his arm. "I'm sure Nick won't mind waiting a few minutes."

"Never mind the tea," Annie said. "What about my toilet? Jennifer, didn't you hear me tell you that it's leaking?"

Had she fallen down a rabbit hole when she'd been out in the garden? Since Nick Lancaster's arrival, it seemed her family had gone crazy. "I'll phone someone to fix it," she promised her aunt. "But I think it can wait until—"

"I could take a look at it," Nick offered. "While you're preparing the tea."

"Thank you, but no. You're a guest. Aunt Annie, could you please pour—"

"I don't mind," Nick insisted. Cleverly, he put his case to her aunt. "I assure you I've had some practice in the area of home repairs. My parents split when I was a teenager and my mother was not mechanically inclined. Fortunately, I had a grand-father who bought me a toolbox and taught me the basics."

"Including leaking toilets?" Annie's keen blue eyes were begging not to be disappointed.

"Including leaking toilets."

"Oh, good," Jennifer said, only just managing not to roll her eyes. "Maybe you can look at the squeaking hinge on the oven door next."

Nick seemed surprised, but quickly nodded. "Sure, that wouldn't be—"

"I was joking! You're a paying guest. I don't want you doing the chores around here." She tried to transmit a reproachful message to Annie, but her aunt was still gazing adoringly at Nick. The old woman's face actually broke into a beam when he took her arm and asked her to lead him to the problem.

Jennifer's father grabbed his cane and followed.

I love my family, Jennifer reminded herself, as she made her way to the kitchen. It was the largest room in the house, and included an eating area where breakfasts were served every morning at eight.

Jennifer had scones for the tea, clotted cream from a nearby dairy and homemade peach-blueberry-lavender preserves. She put on the kettle for tea, then set out her mother's china.

She was slicing a lemon, when she heard someone enter from the hall. Not recognizing the uneven gait of her father, or her aunt's characteristic shuffling, she figured it had to be Nick.

"Finished with the toilet already?"

"It needs a new seal. I'll have to go to a hardware store for supplies. Your father is helping your aunt mop up the floor. He said to tell you they'll be in shortly."

Nick slipped behind the island that separated the kitchen from the seating area. Guests didn't usually stray into her territory, and Jennifer felt her shoulders tighten with the awareness that he was watching her.

"Can I get you something?" she asked, hoping he would take the hint and sit down.

"No, thanks."

Instead, he gravitated to the collage of photographs and postcards on the near side of the fridge. After studying them for about a minute he asked, "When were you in Europe?"

"Six years ago." Jennifer couldn't resist checking over the collection, too. After so many years, you'd think some of the pleasure would have worn thin. But no, just one glance at that photo of her and Simone at the Café Liberté, and she could feel the exciting buzz in her stomach that had stayed with her for the duration of that once-in-a-lifetime trip.

"You look like you were having a good time."

"The best." For three weeks she'd had no one to look after but herself. Simone had let her set the agenda, and they'd hopped a train for a different country on the smallest of whims.

"Who's your traveling companion? You know, she looks a little like—"

"Simone DeRosier? Yes, that's her. She used to spend her summers here on the island." Mentioning her friend, Jennifer grew cautious. She was used to visitors being curious about Simone, and Jennifer had learned long ago to be discreet.

"Really. You knew Simone DeRosier?"

"We were friends, yes."

"And what's this?"

Nick pointed out another photograph, a group shot of the forget-me-not gang the summer before high school graduation.

"Just my friends." Again, she felt a shot of nostalgic warmth. They'd had so much fun in those days. In many ways, those summers together had been the best days of her life.

"I recognize Simone. And this man next to her. I remember him from the papers. Isn't he the guy that—"

"Yes," Jennifer said, before he could put the rest of his thought into words.

"It's kind of spooky to see them standing next to each other like that."

When she'd found out the truth about Emerson, Jennifer had felt the same way. She'd put that photograph aside for a while. But after some time had passed, she'd realized that she didn't want to wipe out her memories.

Yes, Emerson had turned out to be a monster. But once he'd been their friend. She wanted to remember the good things about him, not the bad.

The kettle began to whistle and Jennifer turned from the mementoes of her former life to pour the water into the pot. "This needs to steep for five minutes. If you'd like, I could show you your room now."

Nick's eyes were on her, and the magic she'd felt earlier began to build again. Attraction. Interest. Sexual awareness.

Then his gaze drifted back to the corkboard. "I'm in no hurry. I'd like to hear more about your trip. And your friends. Do you have more photographs?"

She laughed. Did she have more?

There was a whole box full in the attic. "I was always the one lugging the camera around. But you need to get settled after your long trip. I'm sorry things were so chaotic on your arrival. My family can be a little much at times."

Nick smiled at her and she was suddenly experiencing that breathless thing again. He had to stop looking at her this way. It was…unnerving.

"Your suitcase?" she asked, breaking the moment.

Nick's smile turned rueful. "In the back of the Rover. I'll go get it."

She led him back to the entrance then waited while he retrieved his luggage— one very large suitcase and a briefcase that looked as though it contained a laptop computer.

"Up these stairs… Are you okay with that suitcase?"

"Sure. Michele did tell you I was planning to stay for a month?"

She couldn't meet his eyes as she replied, "That won't be a problem."

At the landing she turned left, away from the other two doors. "We have guests staying in both these rooms but they're out exploring for the day."

"Where's your room?"

People often asked her this, and yet the question felt intimate coming from Nick. Again, she felt too self-conscious to look at him as she answered, "We have three bedrooms on the main level. One's an office, then my father and I each have a room."

She opened the door to the suite, which had been added a few years ago. "I hope you'll be comfortable. It's very private up here and you have your own bathroom."

Nick stepped over the threshold, but instead of inspecting the solid wood furnishings or admiring the good-quality cotton bedding, he focused on her.

"Don't apologize for your family. I like them. And I didn't mind about the toilet. Really, I'm glad to help."

He sounded sincere and kind. Considering his looks and his fantastic build, it seemed too good to be true.

There had to be a catch. He probably had a girlfriend—or several—waiting for him at home.

"Let me know if you need anything. And if you'd like some tea, you know where to find it."

"I'll be right down. But I do have one additional request."

"Yes?"

"Would you show me around the island tomorrow?"

Was he serious? She caught her breath, then nodded. "Sure."

She hoped she didn't sound like this was a big deal, but to her it was. She had dated. She'd had boyfriends. One she'd almost married. But none of the guys from her past could measure up to this one. It seemed like her chance at adventure hadn't been lost after all.

NICK HADN'T THOUGHT ABOUT the fact that Jennifer might have photographs. Pictures from Simone's formative years on Summer Island would really complete the middle section of his book. Nick decided that priority number one would be getting her permission to use some of them. It shouldn't be hard. She was clearly taken with him. And it wouldn't be difficult for him to simulate an interest in her.

She was a pretty woman. Easy natured. Naturally kind. Once they'd had a chance to get to know one another, he'd let her know what he was writing about. The sort of person Jennifer was, she'd probably offer to help before he even needed to ask.

After a quick washup, Nick trooped back down for tea, as he'd promised. It didn't take much to charm the aunt. All he had to do was listen to several of her midwife stories. He didn't even need to fake his interest. The stories were actually fascinating.

Jennifer's father was just as easy to connect with. Philip March was a history buff and he was impressed that Nick knew a bit about affairs north of the border.

"Dad owns every book Pierre Berton ever wrote," Jennifer told Nick.

"I've read some of his myself," Nick said. "My favorite was *Flames Across the Border.*"

Philip's eyes gleamed as he leaned back and stretched out his legs. He looked like he was about to start a long-winded conversation, and apparently Jennifer thought so, too, because she patted Nick's arm in a fortifying way, then crossed the room to pour more tea.

Nick's eyes followed her as he listened to her father. She moved gracefully, light and fast on her feet like someone who squeezed a lot into a day. She'd been so reticent earlier, when he'd asked questions about Simone and the other forget-me-not friends. He wondered how long it would take to get her to relax around him.

To trust him.

As she lifted a dainty tea cup to her mouth, he felt a little stab of guilt. He had a feeling the woman was as innocent and naive as she appeared. Which must be why he suddenly felt like the big bad wolf.

Nick rehashed with Philip the political

motivations behind the War of 1812—
the only time in history that Canadians
and Americans had taken up arms against
each other.

Tea stretched out so long, it became
dinner. Jennifer poured tea and refilled the
jars of cream and jelly several times. Two
sisters in their sixties, introduced to him
as Ruth and Eileen Tisdale, returned exhausted and anxious for an early night
after a day spent hiking in Arbutus Grove
Provincial Park.

An hour later, a couple from Vancouver
celebrating their twenty-fifth anniversary,
returned from their dinner at the Owl's
Nest. They were in their late forties, but
they were so vibrant and fit they seemed
much younger. They chatted only briefly,
before disappearing up to their room.

Determined to get Jenn to himself for a
bit, Nick kept talking until he'd exhausted
even Philip March's interest in history.
When Annie announced it was her bedtime,
Jennifer's father reluctantly pulled himself
out of his chair and said his good night, too.

At last Jennifer and Nick were alone.

The house was dark except for the dimmed light from over the table. The only sounds were the groans of old plumbing, the creaking of a house settling for the night.

Jennifer seemed a little uptight as she tapped her fingernails on the scarred wood table. He wondered what would relax her.

"Do you have any music?"

She looked relieved as she got up to turn on the stereo. "What do you like? Rock, country, classical, jazz? We have it all."

"Do you have any of your friend's CDs?" He cursed himself as her shoulders tightened. "But anything jazz would be good," he amended.

She slipped on a disk from another Vancouver artist he recognized: Diana Krall.

"I picked up a case of wine after I crossed the border. How about we open a bottle?"

"That sounds nice."

Encouraged, he ended up bringing in

two bottles and once Jennifer had a glass in her hand, she finally seemed more at ease.

"I like this," he said.

She must have thought he meant the music, because she replied, "Simone used to complain that this CD was too bland."

Nick couldn't have asked for a better opening. "I can see why she would say that. Simone's music really stood out."

Jennifer took another sip of her wine.

Nick hesitated. Decided to give it another try. "Forget Me Not, Old Friend, for instance. That was a real groundbreaker."

The song had catapulted Simone to instant fame. Many critics still considered it the best piece of music she'd ever produced.

Of course one of the reasons the song was so unforgettable was because of the question it posed.

You see a comet cross the sky, you make a wish, it passes by; but will you remember me at the brilliant end?

Forget me not, my one true friend.

Who was the one true friend Simone had been singing about? After years of research, Nick was almost certain it had to be one of the gang from Summer Island.

But which one? Harrison, the ex-husband? Emerson, the man who had been so obsessed with Simone he'd been driven to murder? Gabe, the spurned lover? Aidan, the loyal friend of the husband?

Or Jennifer, Simone's closest—and perhaps only—girlfriend?

Nick knew he couldn't finish his book until he had the answer. But it didn't seem he'd get any clues from Jennifer. At least not tonight. She still hadn't replied to his comment about the forget-me-not song and he worried that he'd get her suspicious if he raised the subject again.

Be patient, Lancaster, he counseled himself. After all, he had a month to get what he needed.

CHAPTER THREE

JENNIFER OPENED HER EYES, certain that the announcer on her radio alarm had made a mistake. It couldn't be quarter to eight. She never slept in.

Morning was the craziest time of Jennifer's day. She usually prepared as much as she could the night before: setting the table, mixing the dough for muffins or scones, filling the coffeemaker with fresh grounds and water so all she'd need to do was press a button in the morning.

But last night she'd done none of that. She and Nick had talked until past midnight. Since she'd been too tired to deal with her usual late-night chores, she'd set the alarm a little earlier for the next morning.

But somehow she'd slept through it.

Jennifer rubbed her eyes, then confirmed the time for herself. Damn. She only had fifteen minutes until she was supposed to serve breakfast to her five guests, plus her father and aunt.

She pulled herself out of her warm, lavender-scented sheets. Winced. Her head ached.

Then she remembered the wine she and Nick had shared last night.

When was the last time she'd had more than one or two glasses? She couldn't remember.

She grabbed jeans and a fresh T-shirt, then slipped out to the bathroom. Sounds of someone cooking came from the kitchen. Miracle of miracles, her father must be up preparing the breakfast. She washed quickly, then hurried out to help him.

"Good morning, Jennifer." Her father peered over his bifocals at her, then blinked as if he couldn't quite focus this early in the morning.

He looked like a crotchety old man with his disheveled gray hair and whiskers bristling on his chin. His lean frame was lost in an oversize sweatshirt and pants that seemed as if they'd fall to the ground given one good tug. But he was definitely her hero this morning.

"Thanks, Dad." She gave him a kiss, then checked the coffee machine. Good, he'd already switched it on. She pulled out place mats, then set the table. Her father tossed a spoonful of salt into a big bowl of batter. "What's on the menu?"

"Pancakes with fresh blueberries. I picked 'em this morning."

"That sounds great." Jennifer pulled out the blender to make smoothies...one of the B and B specials. She grabbed bananas and strawberries from the freezer and blended them with vanilla yogurt and milk.

The first of the guests came into the kitchen just as she was pouring thick smoothies into tall glasses. Steve and Laura Waterton were looking forward to renting kayaks and heading for the Broken Islands. As Jennifer answered their questions about the weather forecast, the Tisdale sisters came down.

"How did you sleep?" Jennifer asked as she poured them each a cup of coffee.

"The birds were dreadfully noisy," Ruth said. "The racket started before dawn."

"I thought the singing was lovely," Eileen said. "We have so few songbirds in the city, anymore. Just robins and sparrows, really. The odd chickadee."

Jennifer wasn't surprised that they each felt differently about the morning birdsong. The sisters seemed to be direct opposites in everything from looks—Ruth was long and lean with angular features, while Eileen was short and plump and pretty—to temperament.

"I suppose I'll have to sleep with the window closed tonight." Ruth slid into the chair with the best view of the gardens.

Eileen, unperturbed by her sister's grumbling, smiled and took the seat across from her sister.

The final guest appeared then. "Good morning, everyone."

Nick's entrance immediately brightened the mood of the room. Jennifer didn't think she was the only one who felt it. Even Ruth managed a smile and a word of welcome.

He helped himself to coffee, then sat at the one remaining place setting. Jennifer passed around glasses of smoothie and when she reached him, he touched her arm.

"When are you free?" he asked.

She felt the blood shoot up to her face. "I need to clean the kitchen and wash a few loads of laundry." The Waterton's room had to be prepared for new guests. "Then I have my morning yoga class. I'm finished around eleven-thirty."

Most afternoons she gardened. But today, she would make an exception.

"I saw the sign to the yoga studio on my drive from the ferry. Orange-and-blue colored building?"

"That's the one."

"How about I pick you up and we go on from there?"

"That would be fine." Fine? Talk about an understatement. She couldn't remember when she'd looked forward to something as much as this. She'd had so much fun talking to him last night. Once they'd gone to their separate rooms, she'd stayed up for hours replaying their conversation. After his awkward question about the forget-me-not song—she always hated when that subject came up—they'd discussed travel. Nick had been to a lot of places. Not overseas, but he'd visited almost every state, as well as much of Mexico and Central America.

She'd drunk in every story, every detail.

"Pancakes are ready," her father announced, bringing a laden platter to the table.

The pancakes were thinner than usual, with crispy edges. A little concerned, Jennifer went to the stove and sampled one of the pancakes still on the griddle.

She couldn't tell what was wrong, but it didn't taste right. She glanced back at the table and watched as Nick lifted a forkful of pancake to his mouth. He chewed, then stopped. A look of mild surprise crossed his face. He reached for his cup of coffee.

"These are different," Steve Waterton said.

"They certainly are." Ruth pinched her mouth and set down her fork.

"I did a little improvising today," her father said proudly, clearly taking the comments as compliments. "Tossed in a few splashes of white wine. What do you think?"

Jennifer's gaze shot to the spot on the counter where she'd left the bottles after her late night conversation with Nick. There'd been about a third of a bottle left when she went to bed, but now both bottles were empty.

At the table, everyone was silent for a moment. Nick scooped more pancake onto his fork. "Very Parisian," he pronounced.

"They say you can add white wine to anything," her father said.

Obviously he'd been watching too many cooking shows.

"That may be true, but I hope you didn't add any to the coffee." Ruth picked up her mug and sniffed the steaming liquid suspiciously.

Her father laughed and Jennifer forced herself to join in, though she strongly suspected Ruth had not meant her comment as a joke.

"Eat up," her father said. "I've got plenty more in the kitchen." He joined her by the griddle, picked up the spatula. "Why don't you sit down at the counter and eat, too, Jennifer? I've got this covered."

She'd been about to suggest she defrost some muffins she kept in the freezer for emergencies. But she could just imagine how her father's face would fall if she did that. He was so pleased with himself, with his efforts to save her the trouble of preparing breakfast for once.

His intentions were good. But why, oh why, couldn't he have followed the recipe that she, and her mother before her, had been using with great success for the past thirty years?

"Thanks, Dad. I'd love some pancakes."

He carefully flipped three onto a plate and handed it to her. "You work too hard, Jennifer. I should handle breakfast for you more often."

"...NINE AND TEN," MOLLY Springfield finished counting, then curled her spine up from the yoga mat and rested her palms on her knees. "That's it for this morning, everyone. Please take your time coming up from the floor."

Molly moved to the back of the room where she gradually brightened the lighting and lowered the thermostat to normal room temperature. She toweled off her face and the back of her neck, then slipped a light, hooded jacket over her bright red sports bra.

A few of the participants were rising now. One of the first, as usual, was Jennifer. She had a lithe body and the postures came to her easily. But she tended to approach each session like a workout, rather than the spiritual refresher it was meant to be.

Observing Jennifer roll up her yoga mat quickly and efficiently, Molly reflected that if anyone needed the relaxing, calming effects of yoga, it was Jennifer. She was always rushing, always busy, too thin, too stressed. She ran the family business practically on her own and had to look after not only her elderly father, but now her aunt, as well.

Then there were her volunteer projects.

Jennifer never turned down anyone who asked for a favor. She was so kindhearted. *Too* kindhearted. A few times now Molly had tried to convince her that she took on too much, but she wouldn't listen. Still, Jennifer was her best friend on the island and Molly did not intend to give up on her.

A gray-haired grandmother of five smiled up at Molly from the floor. Agnes was still fully reclined on her mat, looking refreshed and relaxed. "That was great, Molly. My hips feel so much better since I started coming here."

"I'm glad you made it out today, Agnes."

"Wouldn't miss it. Especially now that all the kiddies are back in school." Agnes rolled onto her side, then gently eased her body into a sitting position. She'd had surgery three months ago, but you'd never know to look at her now.

Though she'd been the first up from the floor, Jennifer waited until all the others had left before she approached Molly.

"Thanks, I needed that."

"Can you stay for a cup of tea?"

Jennifer's cheeks, already rosy, seemed to go hotter. "Not today. Sorry."

"Errands?"

"Um…" Jennifer fussed with the zipper on her sweatshirt.

"Nothing's wrong, is it?"

"No. No."

Molly followed her friend out of the renovated garage to the garden. Across the street the Kincaid's beautiful Victorian home was a familiar, benevolent presence. Molly waved at Justine Kincaid who was sitting on the front porch in a rocking chair. It looked like she was nursing six-month-old Erica. The two of them were alone this week, as Harrison had taken his daughter Autumn to Seattle for the week.

Molly focused on Jennifer again. Sometimes a blunt question was the only way to find out what you wanted to know. "So why can't you stay for tea?"

Jennifer's gaze shifted to the side. "It's just that I have this new guest who wants a tour of the island."

"I hope you're charging for your services."

Jennifer looked at her blankly.

"Come on, Jenn. If you're going to give up an entire afternoon to show this guest around the island, you ought to be properly reimbursed for your time."

Jennifer was still staring at her as if she were speaking in a foreign language. "I never even *thought* of charging him."

Him. Suddenly Molly saw the situation in a new light. "How old is he, Jenn? Is he cute? Is he single?"

As she peppered questions at her friend, Jennifer's cheeks grew brighter than ever. Molly grinned. This was great. Jennifer was going out with a *guy*.

And speaking of the guy, this must be him now, driving up in a dilapidated-looking Land Rover. Molly had an indistinct glimpse of a dark-haired man with a lean face. Then he jumped out of the driver's seat and headed toward them.

"Oh, he *is* cute, Jenn. Yum. He doesn't have a friend or a brother, does he?"

"Molly, it isn't like that," Jenn insisted. Yet, her color wasn't settling down as the man approached.

He was dressed in hiking boots, shorts and a light gray T-shirt. As he drew closer, Molly frowned. He reminded her of someone.

As soon as he spoke, she remembered.

"How was the class, Jennifer? I hope you aren't too tired for our tour?"

Jennifer said something in reply, but Molly didn't hear her. She backed up until she felt the solid wall of her house behind her. Oh my God, she couldn't believe this.

Nick Lancaster. This could not be coincidence. How had he managed to track her to Summer Island?

"THE CLASS WAS GREAT, NICK. Molly's an excellent instructor." Jennifer looked around and was surprised to realize she was now alone in the front yard.

"Molly?" The front door of the cottage was closed. Maybe Molly didn't want to be a third wheel…

Jennifer nearly groaned, remembering Molly's teasing. This wasn't a date, she'd told her friend, but she wasn't sure if Molly had believed her.

It isn't a date, she reminded herself, as Nick moved a little closer. She slipped a hoodie over her tank top, waiting as he checked out Molly's house.

"Why did your friend run inside like that?"

"I'm not sure. I was hoping to introduce you."

"Have you known her a long time?"

"About two years. She moved here from Toronto after her mother died."

"Her mother's dead?"

"Yes." Now why would he have asked that? "She has no family at all anymore."

Nick's expression grew thoughtful. "Summer Island is a long way from Toronto. Why do you suppose she moved here? Did she know anyone?"

"No, but I'm sure glad she did. She's become one of my best friends. Hopefully you'll get a chance to meet her another time."

"I hope so, too."

Jennifer glanced back at Molly's house. It was strange the way she'd disappeared so quickly. But maybe she'd been tired. This had been her third class today.

"So are you ready?" Nick asked.

"Sure."

On the way to the Rover, Nick caught sight of the Kincaids' summer home across the street. Justine had been out on the porch earlier, but she and the baby must have gone inside.

"Wow. That's a nice looking place."

"Yeah, it is." Jennifer hesitated. So many visitors came to Summer Island hoping to get a glimpse inside Simone DeRosier's old summer home that she'd learned to be reticent about pointing it out. But Nick wasn't just another visitor. "Harrison and Justine Kincaid live there."

"Harrison Kincaid. Wasn't he Simone's husband?"

"Yes." Jennifer walked around him to the Rover, and after a pause, Nick followed. Once they were both seated, he seemed in no hurry to get moving.

"Didn't they have a daughter? She would be, what—six or seven?"

"Autumn's eight now. She's thrilled about her new sister. Justine had a baby girl this spring."

"Yes. I'd heard that. You know there's a rumor going around that Autumn has inherited her mother's voice."

Where would he have heard that?

Harrison and Justine usually did an excellent job of keeping Harrison's daughter out of the public eye. Nevertheless, Nick was right. Autumn was tremendously talented. "She's a natural singer and musician. But Harrison won't allow her to perform in public. She's still very young."

Nick turned back for a final glance at Molly's house. He seemed about to ask another question, but apparently changed his mind. He started the engine. "So. Where to first?"

Jennifer felt a thrill of anticipation. It was a sunny, warm day, chock-full of possibilities. "I think we should park at Pebble Beach and walk to town. I can fill you in on the island history on the way."

"Okay. You're the tour leader."

Nick smiled at her, and Jennifer felt the effect right down to the tips of her toes. Maybe this wasn't a date, but she was looking forward to being with Nick. Until it was time to go home and prepare afternoon tea, she was going to pretend she was a young woman without a care in the world.

She directed Nick to Pebble Beach where they parked, then headed straight for the ocean. The beach was strangely deserted for such a fine day. Of course, vacation season was now over and kids were back at school.

As they walked, their shoes crunched on the tiny rocks. "I see why you call this Pebble Beach."

"We don't have sandy shorelines on the island. In a way that's a good thing, because it's helped keep the tourists away. That, plus the complicated ferry system."

"I visited Saltspring Island once many years ago. From what I've seen so far this island is quite different."

"We have similar topography and weather, but that's where it ends. Ask any local—Saltspring is exactly what we don't want to be."

"Why not? It's very popular."

"Sure. And I like to visit Saltspring, too. In fact, I sell my lavender products through one of the craftswomen there. But Summer Island is just more…real. We aren't overrun with tourists and artists and back-to-nature types."

"You don't like tourists and artists and back-to-nature types?"

His teasing smile gave her that light-headed feeling again. "I don't have a problem with them. It's just that they can squeeze out the locals. Most of the people on our island were born here and live here year-round. They're fishermen and farmers and they don't want yuppies coming from the city and clogging our little town with specialty coffee shops and upscale hardware stores."

"So is it an us against them mentality?"

"A little bit," she admitted.

"What about your friends? Harrison Kincaid lives in Seattle, doesn't he? And Simone wasn't a full-time resident, either."

She laughed. "I don't make full-time residency a condition for my friendship." They were on the boardwalk now, the ocean to their right as they headed toward Cedarbrae. How had they ended up talking about her friends again?

She had so many questions to ask him. Last night they'd talked about travels, but nothing personal. She wanted to know everything there was to know about Nick Lancaster. "How long have you been a writer?"

"From the time I could hold a pen in my hand, practically. But I didn't sell my first book until I was twenty-eight. Since then I've been lucky to make a pretty decent living. What about you? I'm assuming you were born and raised here. Did you ever move away for a while?"

"Never." She couldn't help sighing as she said this.

"You didn't go to college or university or anything?"

"I was supposed to. But my mother died the year I graduated high school. I stayed back to help my father adjust…and then he had his stroke. I couldn't leave then."

He paused to throw a rock into the ocean. "You never married?"

"No. But once…I came close." Jennifer didn't think of her aborted engagement very often. She could hardly picture Barry in her mind, or imagine his voice, or the way it had felt to kiss him.

It was hard to believe she'd once considered linking her life with that of a man who had made such a non-lasting impression. "But that was a long time ago."

"What about now?" His gaze swept over her. "Do you have a boyfriend?"

Please don't let me blush again. It didn't mean anything that he was curious. This was the sort of general interest question that people did ask. "No. That's one drawback about living on a small island. Not many single men, especially by the time you get to your thirties. Molly and I sometimes joke about sending away for mail-order husbands."

Nick chuckled, and Jennifer waited for him to offer his own romantic history. When he didn't, she prodded.

"Have *you* ever been married?"

"Never. Though I came close once, too."

"Oh?"

"We lived together for a few years. Then she dumped me."

His smile was self-deprecating and yet so utterly charming that Jennifer felt another twist of her heart. Had he really been dumped? It didn't seem possible. What woman in her right mind would dump Nick Lancaster? There had to be more to his story, but they'd reached the outskirts of Cedarbrae and Derby's Diner was before them.

"I'm kind of hungry," Nick said. "You?"

"Derby's serves a good lunch. Want to give it a try?"

Nick hesitated a moment, then said, "Actually, I was here for lunch yesterday."

"Really? So was I."

"Is that right?" He opened the door for her and they went inside.

CHAPTER FOUR

IN NICK'S EXPERIENCE MOST people loved to talk about themselves. Not Jennifer. He would have found her lack of self-absorption appealing if it hadn't been so counter to his purposes. Every time he managed to orchestrate the conversation around to her life—and her friends' lives—Jennifer quickly steered it back to him.

As they made their way to a booth along the far wall, he took stock of all the Simone DeRosier paraphernalia on display. Yesterday he'd been so focused on Molly and Jennifer that he hadn't noticed the framed photographs and posters.

Despite having seen hundreds of pictures of Simone, and hours of videotape, he was struck anew by how in-your-face beautiful she had been. He wondered if that had ever bothered Jennifer. Most of the women he knew admitted to the odd bit of jealousy. But so far he hadn't caught a glimpse of it in Jennifer.

Was the woman really too good to be true?

"Anything to drink?" The female server was at their table before they'd opened their menus. She looked and sounded a little grumpy, but Jennifer gave her a warm smile anyway.

"I'll have a coffee, please, Josie. Thanks a lot."

The server turned to him and he asked for his usual. "I think I'll have a double latte, no fat, extra hot."

The server gaped. "What?"

He winked at Jennifer. "Just coffee for me, too, please."

The poor woman, now more confused than grouchy shook her head slightly, then walked away, heading for the coffee station next to the kitchen.

"That was mean, Nick, teasing Josie that way."

And yet she was smiling, if rather reluctantly.

"Sorry. Couldn't resist." He liked seeing Jennifer smile, though she was still pretty when she didn't. Yesterday when he'd watched her picking flowers in the garden, he'd had a few moments when he'd actually felt bowled over.

And his reaction had puzzled him. Typically his taste in women ran to urban sophisticates. His ex-fiancée had been—and still was—a senior editor at his publishing house.

Karen was amusing, smart and witty. And, he had to admit it, she'd had a bit of a cruel streak, too. He had a feeling she would have satirized Jennifer's sweet, unassuming ways.

Don't you think it's an act, darling? No one could possibly be that nice.

Yet, she was. He didn't doubt for a minute that Jennifer March was the real deal.

The server came back with their

coffees. Jennifer pushed aside her menu and leaned closer to him. "Do you know what you'd like to eat? The seafood cassoulet is Derby's specialty."

He was more of a burger guy himself, but he nodded. "I'll try it."

Josie nodded, then scurried back to the kitchen. Jennifer leaned closer. "So tell me about your books."

He stifled a groan.

"What are they about? How long does it take you to write one?"

She'd beaten him to the punch. Got the conversation rolling in exactly the wrong direction. Now he had no choice but to talk about the very subject he wanted to avoid. "Every book is different. The last one took three years, including research."

"Is that why you're here? To do research?"

"Yes." Nick made a production of passing Jenn the cream and offering her sugar. Then he took a long drink of his coffee, even though it was so hot it scalded the roof of his mouth.

Of course he was eventually going to have to come clean with what he was doing here and what his book was about. He probably should have done so already. But once he did, she'd be more conscious about what she was telling him. This might be his only opportunity to get some unguarded thoughts and opinions.

Nick smiled and Jennifer's cheeks pinkened again. She was so damned cute and clearly she liked him. Maybe…

No. That was definitely a bad idea. A little flirting, a little fun, sure. But this couldn't go any further than that.

"A few years ago we had another author stay at our B and B," Jennifer said. "Craig Richards. Have you heard of him?"

Great. She was talking about writing again. Nick shook his head.

"He was researching a kayakers' guide to the Gulf Islands. I have an autographed copy of his book in the sitting room."

Nick wondered if Jennifer would want

an autographed copy of *his* book when he was done. It might be fun to come back here after the book was out and sign some copies for the locals…

But he was getting ahead of himself. He had to write the damn thing first. And to do that, he needed facts. Feeling a little like a tennis player trapped in an endless volley, he looked pointedly at the poster of Simone on the wall beside them.

"I guess the locals are pretty proud of their celebrity."

Jennifer's posture tightened. She didn't look at the poster as she said, "Yes, we are."

Why was she so guarded every time he mentioned the famous singer? He pretended not to notice the reaction. "So how did you keep up your friendship after she became famous? She must have been very busy."

"Simone was the kind of person who made things happen. If a hole opened in her schedule, she would be on the phone, arranging things. One day I'd get a call from her, the next I'd be taking the ferry to Vancouver to catch a flight."

"Is that how your Europe trip happened?"

She nodded. "Simone had the idea on a Tuesday and we were in the air a week later. Between trips we stayed in touch with long phone calls."

"All worked around her schedule, of course. Her convenience, her availability."

Jennifer's eyes narrowed. "She had more demands on her time than I did."

Having seen how hard Jennifer worked, Nick doubted that.

"Simone wasn't perfect, but she was my friend. And I loved her."

Maybe she had. She sure seemed sincere. But Nick wondered if he might be getting to the source of all that tension he sensed. The friendship seemed to be more one-sided than Jennifer was prepared to admit. "You must have been devastated when she died."

"It was awful. Especially at first when we believed she'd killed herself."

Emerson had set up his crime to look like suicide. And for over a year, he'd fooled everyone. During that time there must have been a lot of guilt. And all the forget-me-not friends would have felt it. "It must have been torture for her husband…"

"Yes. Harrison took it the hardest."

Nick had figured he would have. "But it was Harrison who eventually proved Simone was murdered, right?"

She nodded. "We all thought he was crazy when he first told us his theory. No one more so than Justine. But it turned out that Emerson was the crazy one and Harrison was right."

"That must have been a real shocker. Had any of you suspected Emerson had these obsessive, romantic feelings for Simone?"

"No. It was always Harrison and Gabe fighting over her, so we were all dumbfounded. But after Emerson killed himself, the RCMP found papers in his house. Apparently in his mind Simone had loved him more than anyone else in the world. When he got up his nerve to tell her he loved her and wanted her to leave Harrison, and she refused, he killed her, then staged the scene to look like suicide. I still can't believe it."

Jennifer wasn't even looking at him as she spoke. Clearly she was reliving the past, still trying to come to grips with the horrible death of her friend.

Poor Jennifer. He felt sympathy for her, and that worried him. It would be crazy for him to let his conscience get in the way now. This was good stuff. He had to keep her talking.

"That wasn't the first time Emerson committed murder, was it?"

"No. Years ago he killed his parents."

The articles Nick had read had alluded to past homicides but had been hazy with details. He leaned forward to catch every detail of Jennifer's answer.

"It was so cold-blooded and…and *senseless*, Nick. They wanted to retire. That was all. That's why he killed them."

"But what did their retirement matter to him?"

"They were going to sell the landscaping company and use the proceeds to buy a place in Arizona. Emerson had worked at the family business all his life."

"So it was about money?"

"That's right. For the sake of a few hundred thousand dollars, Emerson rigged the brakes in the family car and his parents died in a horrible accident."

The color of her eyes grew more intense, thanks to a sudden pooling of tears. Jennifer brushed them away. "But here I am babbling about people you don't even know. You must be bored."

Nick cleared his throat. It was time to come clean. He drew the line at *lying*.

"Actually, Jennifer, I do—"

"Two specials," Josie announced, arriving at their table with a tray.

Nick sat back in his chair to give her room to unload the plates. Jennifer was smiling at the woman again, chatting about local politics. When the server finally left, the moment was lost.

He'd have to wait for another opportunity to discuss Simone DeRosier and the forget-me-not friends again.

AFTER LUNCH, JENNIFER GAVE Nick the full-blown tour. The island had been explored by the Spanish and the British in the 1700s, but wasn't settled until the 1850s. Most of the residents worked in small businesses or as farmers or fishermen. Logging wasn't permitted anywhere on the island, so except for a few cultivated areas, the rain forest remained majestic and untamed.

As they drove leisurely along the main road that circled the island, Jennifer enjoyed sharing her knowledge of the place she'd called home all her life. It was strange how proud she was of a place that sometimes felt like a prison to her.

But the isolation was a big part of the island's charm. Though they weren't far, as the crow flies, from the mainland, the combined ferry crossings meant that it took over half a day to travel to either Vancouver or Victoria, the two nearest cities. And because Summer Island was so lightly populated, even during high season the ferry only ran two times a day. If you were late...you were stuck where you were until the next scheduled crossing.

"Arbutus Grove Park." Nick read aloud the sign on the side of the road, automatically slowing the Rover's speed at the same time. "Wow, look at those trees."

The diameter of some of the cedars spanned ten feet or more. Then there were the arbutus, rare broad-leafed evergreens with smooth dark red wood. This was the largest preserved grove of arbutus in all the Gulf Islands.

"This forest is our equivalent to the Queen's crown jewels. Want to stop and hike down to the ocean?"

"Sounds like a plan."

Nick took her arm as she stepped out of the vehicle, and he kept hold of her hand as they settled on one of the paths that promised a two-kilometer scramble to the rocky shoreline.

"Watch your step," Nick said as they came across a fallen tree in their path.

He was a courteous companion. Charming. Good company. He'd paid the check for their lunch without her even noticing. And easy to talk to. Jennifer couldn't remember the last time she'd babbled so much.

He seemed interested in all of it. Her happy, carefree childhood. Aunt Annie's previous life as a midwife. Her father's attempts to retain his independence, even though the stroke had robbed him of most of the strength on his left side.

He was wonderfully attentive. The only problem was, whenever she asked a question of him, he wasn't nearly as forthcoming as she would have liked.

It would be exaggerating to label him secretive… but not by much. She decided to try again. "Have you always lived in New York City?"

"Born and raised."

She felt a little envious of that. Every time she'd visited Simone there, she'd loved the city. But she'd felt out of her element, too. She suspected no one who hadn't grown up there could ever feel like they really belonged in a place like New York City.

"It's hard to imagine a place more different from New York than Summer Island. It must seem very dull here to you."

Jennifer was having a good time with Nick, but she couldn't get a read on the man. There were moments when he withdrew into himself and appeared a little cool and distant. But mostly he seemed to enjoy being around her as much as she enjoyed being with him.

In fact, there were times, like now, when she caught a glimpse of something more in his eyes.

"Jennifer?" He pulled gently on her arm, forcing her to stop walking and look at him. "Nothing I've seen on Summer Island so far has seemed dull to me."

She swallowed, trapped in place by the power of his gaze. A slow heat started at her core and began to build. The world collapsed into one small area…the space between him and her.

And then that space began to shrink as he lowered his head and wrapped his arms around her.

"Jennifer?"

She could hardly breathe. "Yes?"

He didn't have an answer. Only a kiss. And while she'd been expecting it, she hadn't expected to feel so much from it. The wine last night hadn't been nearly this intoxicating. She went up on tiptoe and settled her hands tentatively on the firm platform of his shoulders.

His lips brushed softly over hers, settling on her cheek, then her ear, then the side of her head.

More, she wanted to demand. *I need more.*

But he let her go. He turned his face to the side, looking just a tad guilty. He probably hadn't planned for that kiss to happen. Now he was worried she was going to read too much into it.

She took a step away from him. "Well. That wasn't supposed to be part of the tour."

They laughed uneasily, then continued walking.

"You're sure you don't have a boyfriend who's going to punch my lights out for doing that?"

"No boyfriend. Not in a long time. Wait. That makes me sound just a little pathetic, doesn't it?"

"Not at all. At least I hope not since I'm not in a relationship right now, either. But what about the guy you almost married? Does he still live on the island?"

"No. He never did. It was a long-distance thing and it happened a long time ago. His name was Barry Collins."

"Barry Collins. I feel like I've heard that name before. Should I have?"

Only if he read the fine print in the movie magazines. But surely a man like Nick wouldn't waste his time with reading material like that.

"I met Barry through Simone. She introduced us after one of her concerts. Looking back, I can see our relationship was doomed to fail. We had nothing in common."

"But he asked you to marry him. So things must have been pretty serious between the two of you. What went wrong?"

She hesitated, not sure how to put it. Everyone here knew the entire story, but Nick didn't need the long version. "I found out I couldn't trust him."

Something dark flashed in Nick's eyes. "Did he hurt you?"

"The details don't really matter. Like I said, it was all ages ago." Barry Collins represented a period of her life that she didn't like to think back on. What was the point? Best to move on and concentrate on the positive. That was the attitude she always tried to take.

"There's the beach." She pointed ahead, using an evasive technique on him for a change.

"Some beach." The shoreline was raised about ten feet from the water's edge and this was high tide. He pulled Jennifer close again.

"You didn't answer my last question," he said.

Their faces were almost as close as they'd been in the moment before he'd kissed her. Jennifer dampened her lips, then took a breath for courage before she could force herself to meet his gaze. "You've been avoiding my questions, too."

"Not true."

"Yes, you have." She loved looking at him, watching the various emotions play upon his face. He had a very expressive mouth. Right now it was being held firmly in check, as if he didn't want so much as a facial twitch to give him away.

"What do you want to know, Jennifer?"

The hint of playfulness that had been in his eyes earlier was gone. She took his free hand in hers and held on tightly, afraid that she might be venturing into territory she'd rather not know about.

"Start with your book, Nick. Tell me what you're writing about."

CHAPTER FIVE

IT SEEMED TO TAKE FOREVER for Nick to answer Jennifer. He opened his mouth a couple of times, before the words finally came out.

"I'm writing a biography," he said.

Right away Jennifer knew.

She felt as if a cold wind had suddenly swept in from the Pacific. Wrapping her arms around her midsection, she stepped backward.

"It's about Simone." Her voice sounded flat. Lifeless. Once again, she couldn't look at him.

Why hadn't she seen this coming? She'd been crazy to think a man like him would be interested in her.

Jennifer picked up the trail and started

back for the road, walking a lot faster than she had on the way down here.

She should have figured this out from the start, from the moment he'd asked her about her trip to Europe with Simone. Many of their guests expressed an interest in her former friendship with the superstar. But there'd been something a little pushy about the way Nick had invaded her space in the kitchen, about the way he had posed his questions. He'd been interested, all right, but at the same time careful not to appear *too* interested

He'd been the same way when she'd shown him the Kincaid house, then again at the restaurant when he'd used Simone's framed photographs as an opportunity to ask more questions.

She'd been so gullible. Never suspecting that he was using her.

She thought back to his arrival at the B and B. That intense moment they'd shared before her father and her aunt had interrupted. Had that been real?

Or had he been acting even then?

"That's why you booked at our B and B. You knew I was her friend. You deliberately targeted me. Then charmed me." She felt so *foolish*. So naive.

"I didn't lie. I just…withheld a little information. I was under no obligation—"

"Oh, give me a break, Nick." Were his moral standards really that low? Or did he think she was so desperate for male companionship that he could convince her his motives weren't suspect?

"How did you find out about me? Lots of reporters have come to the island to write about Simone. None of them have ever tracked me down before."

"It was Simone who led me to you. She mentioned her friend Jennifer in a little interview she did for *Vanity Fair* once."

Jennifer knew the article he was talking about. In answer to one of the questions, about where she'd been happiest, Simone had talked about Summer Island and the friends she had made there. She'd referred to Jennifer as the sister of her heart.

Jennifer had been unbelievably touched

when she'd read that. But how had Nick traced her from that? "She didn't mention my last name. Or where I lived."

"True. But I took a guess you might still be on Summer Island. Turned out I was right."

She needed a moment to absorb that. "You've obviously done a lot of research."

"This is going to be an in-depth biography. Not like that fluffy coffee table book they put out a few months after her death."

"I thought that was a beautiful book." She had a copy at home. The book tracked the highlights of Simone's career, with lovely glossy photographs and snippets of Simone's lyrics throughout. It was a fitting tribute to an amazing musician.

"Simone was an intriguing, complicated woman, who achieved extraordinary success in a very competitive field. Don't you think her life warrants a more in-depth look?"

He looked so earnest, like he really thought she would buy in to this project of his. But the last thing she wanted was someone digging into the details of Simone's life. When reporters and journalists started digging, you could be sure they were only looking for one thing.

Dirt.

And Jennifer didn't want anything to do with that. She knew there had been dark spots in Simone's life. She also knew that Simone had not been perfect, that her flaws had been bigger than life in the same way that her attributes had been.

By why expose all that to the public? What was to be gained?

She recalled his questions from when they'd been in the diner, and realized what this was really about. "It's the murder, isn't it?"

"What do you mean?"

"That's why you want to write this book. Because Simone was murdered. It isn't about her talent or her achievements at all."

"That's not fair. Yes, the murder is part of the fascination. You have to wonder what it was about Simone that caused so

many people—her murderer included—
to become obsessed by her."

"Actually, no, I don't wonder about that.
What you don't seem to appreciate is that
her death was hard for the people who
loved her. We don't want to relive the experience so you can share the sordid details in your book."

"I wouldn't put it that way."

"No, I'm sure you wouldn't." She
tripped over a root and quickly rebalanced
herself, jerking back from Nick's efforts
to steady her. "Don't touch me."

"Sorry. I thought you were going to fall.
Anyway, the murder is only part of it. I'm
also curious about what it was that drove
her ambition. She had what half the popu-
lation of North America secretly longs for."

"And she deserved it. She was very
talented."

"But that's only part of the equation,
don't you think?"

She refused to let him engage her in his
speculation. She wasn't going to be a part
of this. Not at all. Nick's vehicle was in

sight now and she quickened her pace. "I need to get home. It's almost time for tea."

"I'll take you back. But just look at me for a minute, okay?"

She didn't stop until she reached the Rover. Stiffly, she turned to face him. "Well?"

"I want to tell the truth about Simone DeRosier. Is that so awful?"

"Yes." To her it was awful. She didn't want to think about the things Nick was talking about. Obsession and ambition. Simone had been so much more than that.

"I don't understand."

"What don't you get, Nick? That Simone was my friend? That I want to remember the good things about her life, not the bad?" She grasped the handle to the Rover then yanked the door open and stepped up into her seat. Through the open window, Nick studied her face.

"You're afraid."

She turned away.

"Who are you really trying to protect here, Jennifer?"

He didn't, he *couldn't* know what he was saying. "What about Harrison? Her daughter? Have you thought about them or even considered how a tell-all biography might be wounding and hurtful to people who have already suffered so much?"

"Nobody has to read the book if they don't want to."

She couldn't believe him. "Oh, sure."

As if it could be that easy. The publication of this book would create a media frenzy. He'd be on every TV show from *Larry King Live* to *Oprah*. Then there would be the newspaper coverage, excerpts of the book published in various magazines. No matter where Harrison and Autumn turned, they'd be confronted with the public airing of their family's intimate history.

And so would she...

"Jennifer, my goal isn't to hurt anyone." He paused a moment. "This biography will be as complete and truthful as I can make it. And...I was hoping I would have your cooperation."

She blistered him with a glare. "Do you always kiss the girls to make them talk, Nick?"

He groaned. "I'm sorry. I didn't plan on that."

"Oh, really? So you were suddenly so overcome by desire that you forgot I happened to be the best friend of the woman you're writing about?"

"It looks bad, I know, but—"

"Just get in and drive, Nick," she said wearily. "I really do need to get home."

He kicked at a piece of wood on the mossy ground, then walked around to the driver's side. He got into the Rover, and started down the road. "You know, if I don't write this book, someone else will."

"Sure, Nick." Maybe someone would, eventually, write that book. But did it have to be the man who'd just kissed her and made her feel like she was falling in love for the second time in her life?

Or maybe the first.

The truth was, kissing Barry had never been as thrilling as kissing Nick. With hindsight, Jennifer had to wonder if she'd even loved Barry. She'd been flattered at his interest, thrilled with all the travel and the exciting parties and film premieres he'd taken her to in L.A.

But she couldn't remember longing to be alone with him. Talking for hours and feeling like she'd never have enough time to tell him everything that was in her heart.

And for sure she'd never felt the instant, heady explosion of emotion that people called love-at-first-sight. She'd thought that sort of reaction belonged in movies.

Nick Lancaster had put some sort of spell on her. Winning her over completely, when he had absolutely no genuine feeling on his side. And she'd made it so easy for him, practically swooning with all the attention. What were her friends always saying? She was too trusting, too giving.

Well she'd learned her lesson this afternoon, hadn't she?

Jennifer held her head stiffly and kept her gaze fixed ahead. Fifteen minutes later, Nick pulled up to Jennifer's pickup on the side of the road. The Rover had barely stopped when Jennifer opened the door.

"Look, Jennifer, I'm sorry, okay? I'm not just a cheap journalist, hoping to make money off someone else's fame. This is going to be a serious book."

"I'm sure it is, Nick. But right now all I wish is that I could talk you out of writing it."

"That's not going to happen."

Her mouth hardened. "Then you might want to find somewhere else to stay while you're on Summer Island. Because as far as I'm concerned, you aren't welcome at Lavender Farm anymore."

FRANKIE, THE BAKER'S skinny wife, sliced a baguette and stuffed it with turkey, cheese and veggies. "Extra lettuce, the way you like it."

"Thanks, Frankie." Molly picked up a newspaper from a rack near the counter, then sat at one of the little tables. Instead of reading the paper, though, she gazed out the window as she took the first bite of her sandwich.

Only a few minutes passed before she saw him. Gabe stepped out of the *Chronicle* office front door, then loped across the street toward the bakery. She dipped her head over the front page of the *Chronicle* as he entered.

Gabe went up to the counter, where Frankie had his usual ham and Swiss waiting for him. He paid, then turned around and scanned the tables. Though her head was still bent over the paper, she could sense the moment his gaze lit on her.

"Molly."

There was a mixture of mild surprise and pleasure in his voice that made her heart beat just that little bit faster. Oh, but she was a fool.

"May I join you?"

She smiled, then folded the paper into quarters. "Please do. I was hoping to talk to you about a business matter actually."

She'd met Gabe Brooke the first week she'd arrived on Summer Island. After touring the island, and falling in love with it, she'd gone to the real estate office to inquire about buying a cottage.

She'd wanted him the moment she laid eyes on him. And not just to act as her real estate broker. But he'd been too busy to help her and so he'd referred her to Justine. Probably it had been just as well, because he'd been married to Nessa Kincaid at that time.

But as Molly had quietly stood on the sidelines, that marriage had dissolved. Now, two years after they'd separated, with Nessa happily remarried, the coast couldn't be more clear. Yet though Molly sensed Gabe was attracted to her, something still stood in the way.

Was he hung up on Nessa? Worse, maybe it was Simone. The few times he'd talked about the famous singer, Molly had seen the regret in his eyes.

But Gabe was still in his thirties. Young, with so much to live for. Surely he didn't intend to pine over lost love for the rest of his days.

Not that it should matter to her, either way. Not now that Nick Lancaster was on the island. It was inevitable that he would have eventually made his way here. She should have been expecting it.

And consequently should have left long ago.

This had never been intended to be a permanent move. Originally she'd come for just a visit, to learn a little more about Simone and make sure Autumn was okay.

Yet, she'd ended up falling in love with the place. Buying a house. Starting up a business. All of which would have been wonderful, except that her next-door neighbor and her best friend were two of the original forget-me-not friends and she couldn't even tell them who she really was.

"Did you sell that house you were talking about last week?" she asked.

"Yes, but it wasn't easy." Gabe talked about work for a while. Then he asked about her yoga. "One day I'm going to drop in on one of your classes."

The light in his eyes was teasing, his smile slightly flirtatious. She smiled in kind.

"I'd like that."

"Would I have to wear one of those ridiculous outfits?"

She chuckled at the mental picture. Most men *would* look a little silly in yoga pants. But not Gabe. Gabe wore everything with confidence and style. He was just that sort of guy.

Gabe swallowed the last of his sandwich. "So what was this business matter you wanted to discuss?"

She took a deep breath. "I'd like to put my cottage back on the market. I was wondering if you would help me with that."

"Well, the market it hot right now. It could be a good time to trade up."

She wasn't interested in trading up but moving on. But before she could explain, Gabe was standing, brushing crumbs from his cotton shirt.

"I have a one o'clock meeting that I can't be late for. How about you come into my office tomorrow and we talk about this in detail?"

"Sure. That would be fine." They set a time, then Molly slung her purse over her shoulder and left the bakery with Gabe. They parted ways just outside the front door.

As she strolled toward her car, Molly could sense Gabe watching after her.

What a shame that they hadn't just a little more time. She really felt like he could have been the one.

CHAPTER SIX

THAT AFTERNOON THE TISDALE sisters joined Jennifer, her father and her aunt for tea. Predictably Eileen gushed over everything from the flaky scones to the delicious preserves, while Ruth sighed with disappointment.

"Not quite the standard that you'd find at the Empress. But not bad, either," Ruth pronounced.

"Well, I think it's absolutely wonderful."

Did Eileen ever tire of neutralizing her sister's criticisms with compliments? Jennifer took a sip of the tea; a blend her aunt had concocted. She agreed with Eileen. Having had tea at the Empress Hotel in Victoria, she couldn't see that it was in any way superior to this.

"You must admit the Empress is very posh," Ruth countered, returning her cup to its saucer.

"Perhaps. But I'd far rather be here where we can look out over lavender gardens and green pastures. Aren't the sheep adorable, Ruth?"

"They do look white and fluffy from a distance. But I imagine up close they're quite dirty."

Jennifer pretended to dab something from the corner of her mouth to hide her smile. Her father and aunt were talking quietly between themselves, having decided to tune out the sisters' persistent bickering.

Later, as she cleaned the kitchen after the tea, the phone rang. It was Justine, and she sounded distraught.

"Jennifer, I'm in a bind. Harrison and Autumn are in Seattle this week and I've got a client who has made a special trip to the island to view properties. He only has tonight and tomorrow morning to look."

Before she'd married Harrison, Justine

had been a full-time Realtor. Now she worked reduced hours, but by the very nature of her business, those hours were not predictable.

"Usually I can count on Nessa to help me," Justine continued.

Harrison's sister owned the only day care on the island. She and her new husband Dex also had a foster son of their own, but despite all the children running around their home, they were always happy to open their door to one more.

"But Nessa had to close the day care for the rest of the week because Tyler has the chicken pox. They were over for dinner on Saturday and the very next morning he woke up covered in sores."

"Poor Tyler." Jennifer and her family had a soft spot for the little boy. Last summer Annie had helped rescue him from an abusive home situation.

"He's not that sick, Nessa says. But he is contagious." Justine sighed.

Jennifer knew Justine was waiting for her to offer to take the baby. She thought of the bread she needed to bake tonight, the sheets that required ironing.

On the other hand, Justine was a good friend and Erica was a very sweet baby.

"It's no problem," she said. "I can watch Erica for you."

"Oh, Jennifer, you're an angel. Um…is there any possibility she could stay the night, too? I've worked with this couple before and I'm guessing we'll be late. Erica goes to bed around eight and sleeps through the night. You won't even know she's there."

But what about the morning? The breakfast rush? Jennifer hesitated. "Mornings are pretty hectic here… Oh, what the heck. Sure, Erica can stay."

"I'm so sorry to have to ask you for this favor. I know you're full at the B and B. I swear I'll come and help you in your gardens for a full day next week to make it up to you."

Jennifer laughed. "I'm overrun with weeds right now. You've got a deal."

She swung a leg over a bar stool and

settled her weight for a moment. It was almost seven o'clock and Nick still hadn't returned to the B and B. Was he taking her at her word and trying to find another place to stay?

If so, she doubted he'd be successful. Even during September the B and B's, as well as the campgrounds at Arbutus Park, were usually fully booked.

She couldn't picture him giving up though and returning to New York without completing the research for his book. Which meant he'd soon be contacting the rest of the forget-me-not gang.

She had to warn her friends.

"Since I have you on the line, Justine, there's some news I'd like you to pass on to Harrison and Nessa. Could you tell them that a man by the name of Nick Lancaster is on the island. He's staying here and he's writing a book. It's a biography about—"

"Let me guess." Justine sighed. "Simone."

Jennifer knew the singer had never been one of Justine's favorite people. Nor had she been Nessa's. In all honesty, Jennifer knew they had their reasons.

"This isn't going to be a coffee table book like the other one, Justine. I'm pretty sure Nick is going to be interviewing all the old forget-me-not friends. I just thought I should give you a heads-up."

"This was bound to happen eventually," Justine said. "It's the price of celebrity in the modern world."

"I know. But still, the timing sucks. Everyone from the old gang finally has their lives in order again." In just two years there had been three weddings: Harrison and Justine's, Aidan and Rae's, and just a few months ago, Nessa and Dex had finally tied the knot, too.

"Not quite everyone, Jenn. Have you forgotten about Gabe?"

Justine made a good point. Gabe still wasn't on speaking terms with most of the old gang. Harrison had never forgiven him for marrying his younger sister when he was really in love with Simone. And anyone Harrison was angry with, Aidan was angry at, too.

"That's true. I do worry about Gabe. But right now I'm more concerned about Nick Lancaster. I think we should all make a pact not to help him in any way."

"Isn't that a little…extreme? Jenn, I've heard of Nick Lancaster. He's a very reputable author. I'm sure he'll take a balanced approach with his book."

How could she be so calm about this? "Think about Autumn. She was so traumatized after Simone's death. I'd hate to see her regress."

"She won't," Justine said firmly. "We'll make sure of that. So try not to worry, okay? I'll talk to Harrison. He'll know how to deal with this."

"Okay. That sounds good." The unofficial leader of the group, Harrison could be counted on to keep his head in an emergency. Jennifer was pretty sure she could count on him to clamp down on the others where Nick was concerned. "What time will you be bringing Erica over?"

"I just need to organize a few things." From the scuffling sounds over the line, it sounded as if Justine was already packing. "We'll be there in about half an hour."

As soon as she was off the phone, Jennifer hurried to mix the dough for tomorrow's cinnamon buns, then she went to the laundry room to iron sheets. Twenty minutes later, Justine drove up with Erica tucked safely in an infant carrier in the backseat of her immaculate Lexus. Justine's thick strawberry-blond hair was clipped back and she was wearing a sleek-looking silk suit and high heels.

"You look wonderful." Jennifer had never had the sort of job that required her to dress up. She wondered if it would be possible for her to look as professional and polished as Justine did right now.

And her car was just as spotless. Jennifer peeked inside the window. No crumbs or signs of spilled juice on the leather seats.

"How do you keep everything so clean?"

"You should have seen me an hour ago. I had burped-up breast milk all over my shirt. Not a pretty sight, let me tell you." She handed six-month-old Erica to Jennifer then unloaded a portable cot, high-chair and stuffed diaper bag from the car.

"She doesn't travel light, I'm afraid." Justine grinned as she lugged the last of the bags into the house.

Jennifer jiggled the baby on her hip and Erica gave her a big smile. "I think she remembers me."

"I'll set up this cot, then be on my way. Her bottle is ready to go in that side compartment of the diaper bag."

"I thought you were still breast-feeding?"

"I am. I express some every day and keep a supply in my freezer. In the bag you'll find another bottle for the morning, and a third in case of emergency. Here, let me pop this one in some warm water."

Justine ran through the full list of instructions, then handed Jennifer a sheet of paper with everything written out, including Justine and Harrison's cell phone numbers.

"I have to run now. I think it will be easier if you distract her while I leave." She handed Jennifer a book and the heated bottle.

Jennifer carried Erica to the office where Justine had set up the portable cot. She sat on the pullout sofa and opened the book. Erica clapped her hands, delighted.

Half an hour later, the bottle was empty, the story had been read and Erica was fast asleep on her back in the cot.

"Nothing to it," Jennifer congratulated herself quietly. She slipped out of the room, leaving the door ajar, then went to find her father and aunt.

They'd just returned from their evening walk and were settling in the living room with sandwiches. Her father held up one of the squares when he saw her.

"I made one for you, too, Jenn. It's on the kitchen counter. What's with the high chair? Does one of our new guests have a baby?"

She explained about Erica, ignoring her aunt's raised eyebrows and pointed look. Annie, like many of her friends, was always telling her she needed to learn how to say no.

Feeling a little hungry, she went to grab her sandwich. Breakfast was their biggest meal of the day and since they had a full tea around four-thirty in the afternoon, in the evening they usually had a snack like this. She took her tuna on rye back to the living room and settled into one end of the sofa.

Her father was in his recliner, Annie in the chair that had once been her mother's. Ironically enough they were watching *Biography*. The current program was profiling a popular female actress.

When a commercial came on, Jennifer set down her sandwich. "Dad, I found out today that Nick Lancaster is writing a book about Simone."

"Is that right?" Her dad didn't glance away from the TV.

"I'm not really comfortable having him stay here. I was thinking of asking him to leave." Okay, so she'd already asked him. But she was sure her dad would agree with whatever she decided. "We have a waiting list of people for that suite," she added.

"But I like Nick," Annie protested. "And he fixed my toilet this morning. What do we care if he's writing a book about that famous friend of yours?"

"I don't think it's going to be a very flattering portrayal."

Her father frowned. "He seems like a good fellow to me. I don't see a problem with having him here."

"Simone was my best friend, Dad. I don't want to see her memory tarnished."

Annie clucked her disagreement. "You put too much stock in those memories of yours. Yes, Simone was your friend, but she was also a celebrity. It's inevitable that people are going to want to write and read about her. You should be glad that the person tackling the project is someone like Nick."

Jennifer didn't know what to say. Her own family didn't understand how she felt. But then she'd always suspected her father hadn't approved of her friendship with Simone. Probably he'd worried the superstar would turn her head, make her forget who she was and where she came from.

"I wish you would reconsider, Dad. For my sake."

"Seems to me like Nick is going to write that biography wherever he stays." Finally her Dad pulled his gaze from the TV and studied her face. "Is something else going on here, Jennifer?"

It was her turn to look intently at the television. Perhaps she could convince her father to turn Nick out if she told him how Nick had deceived her...and stolen that kiss. But she didn't relish rehashing that experience. She could feel her cheeks growing hot just thinking about it.

"The suite was reserved for Nick months ago," her father concluded. "I can't see turning away a paying guest just because he's writing a book about someone you used to know."

He turned up the volume on the television and Jennifer knew the subject was closed. When her sandwich was done, she returned to the kitchen to punch down the sweet, spongy dough she'd mixed earlier. She preheated the oven then sifted together sugar and cinnamon and set out some butter to soften.

She was getting out the rolling pin when she remembered she still had a load of towels on the line. It was almost dark, and as she stepped outside she could smell rain in the air.

Quickly she unpegged the towels, then carried the full laundry basket inside. She spritzed each towel with lavender water, then folded it and added it to the growing stack. These would go into the upstairs washrooms tomorrow.

As she worked, Jennifer wondered when Nick was finally going to show up. Even if he'd managed the impossible and had found himself another place to stay on the island, he'd still need to come by for his luggage. His laptop was upstairs, too, along with a portable file box, no doubt full of damnable facts about Simone.

What would she say to him when he finally did show? She should think up the perfect cutting remark, something that would hurt him as much as he'd hurt her this morning.

Or no, maybe she should just play it cool, make it clear to him that his kisses hadn't meant anything to her, that she'd considered him merely a diversion...

Oh, who was she kidding? She'd never carry off either approach. He'd hurt her feelings deeply and one look at her face would tell him as much.

Jennifer rolled out the dough, slathered it with butter and sprinkled the spiced sugar on last. She rolled it into a cylinder, brushed the exterior with more melted butter and sugar, then rolled the log in a mixture of sunflower, sesame and flax seeds. With a sharp knife she sliced off two-inch-fat buns and set them on a tray to rise again.

As she was grinding coffee for the

morning pot, she heard a commotion at the front door. She stepped out to the hall and welcomed the Tisdale sisters back from their evening outing. They settled on the sofa to watch the news and she put out hot water for tea and biscuits to go with it.

Back in the kitchen she poured fresh water into the coffeemaker and set the breakfast table with her mother's china. As she was finishing up, the young couple who had moved into the Watertons' old room returned.

Still no Nick. He knew they locked the front door at midnight. All guests were informed of this policy when they registered. He hadn't somehow snuck past her and removed his belongings, had he?

Jennifer ran upstairs to check, but his room was as he had left it that morning. His suitcase lay empty on the floor and the computer and several files of papers were on the desk.

She resisted the temptation to peek through those papers and retreated back downstairs. All their guests had retired for the night and the sitting room was empty now. She gathered the dirty teacups and plates and hand washed them in the old-style farmer's sink.

Ten minutes until midnight.

Where was Nick?

The rain started, a gentle, soothing sound. Jennifer loved the rain. So why did she suddenly feel so empty? So alone?

She sank back onto the stool, lowering her head to the counter. The CD player next to the toaster switched from one song to the next. She turned off the machine and in the ensuing silence she heard the front door open.

It was one minute to midnight and Nick had finally returned.

JENNIFER MET HIM IN THE foyer, leaving plenty of space between them. "You're back."

"Is that okay?"

She smelled like cinnamon and lavender, and several strands of long blond hair had escaped her ponytail. She looked delicious in every sense of the word and he wondered how he was going to survive the next four weeks without kissing her again.

"An honorable man wouldn't ask. He would just check out and leave quietly."

"But you already know I'm not honorable, right, Jenn?"

She met his gaze and held it, and in her eyes he saw hurt behind the anger. "Look, I'm sorry for what happened today. I should have told you what I was doing sooner. And that kiss…" He shook his head. "That was just an impulse. Maybe a stupid one."

Definitely a stupid one. What had he been thinking? Yeah, he'd wanted to charm her a little. But kiss her? That wasn't the way he usually operated.

"So…is your dad waiting at the top of the stairs with a shotgun?"

Reluctantly she shook her head. "He likes you. He wants you to stay."

That was a welcome surprise. He guessed Jennifer hadn't told him about the kiss.

"Aunt Annie does, too. Apparently, you're spectacular with toilets."

"My claim to fame." He shifted weight from one foot to the other, tired from his long day of pounding pavement. He must have talked to every shop owner in Cedarbrae today. Fortunately not everyone on Summer Island shared Jennifer's reticence to speak about the famous Simone. "What about you, Jenn? How did you vote at the family council?"

She shrugged. "In this case, majority rules. I'm not going to insist that you leave."

"So, I'm staying on sufferance?"

"You're lucky to be staying at all. If it was just up to me, you wouldn't be."

He sighed. "I take it you aren't going to accept my apology?"

"I'm not going to help you with your book, Nick. And I've already warned my friends not to help you either."

"Yeah?" Damn, he'd really alienated her with his charm and disarm strategy. But he'd never guessed she'd go so far as to unite her friends against him. "Should I thank you for being honest?"

"Here's some more honesty. You really should consider going back to New York City. You're not going to find out anything useful for your book on this island."

"You think?"

"I *know*."

He'd dealt with this sort of attitude before. Not everyone welcomed putting their lives under the biographer's microscope. Clearly Jenn was one of those types.

But it was curious. Why was she so protective where Simone and her friends were concerned?

"Fair enough, Jenn. Can I be honest in return?"

She looked at him, waiting.

"Whether you and your friends help me or not, I'm still writing this book. And I won't be checking out until my entire month is up."

CHAPTER SEVEN

TWO HOURS LATER, Jennifer awoke from a deep sleep, feeling disoriented. What was that sound?

Crying.

And then she remembered. Erica. The baby was sleeping in the room across the hall. She had to get up and see what was wrong.

But Jennifer's head felt as if it had been weighted down with bricks. She had no practice with getting up at two in the morning. It sure wasn't easy.

Somehow she stumbled to her feet and threw on a robe. She crossed the hall to the office and found Erica standing in her cot, clutching the side.

"Hey, sweetie, what's the matter?"

Erica looked startled, then cried louder. Jennifer picked her up and cuddled her. "I'm sorry I'm not your mom. Hey, you feel a little warm."

Jennifer put a hand on the baby's forehead. It was definitely warm.

Oh no. Could the baby have chicken pox, too? Justine had mentioned something about Nessa, Dex and Tyler being over for dinner, so Erica could have been exposed.

Jennifer was immediately wide awake with worry. Still holding Erica close, she dug around in the diaper bag. In one of the pouches she found medical supplies, including infant pain reliever and a thermometer, the kind that registered temperature from the ear.

She'd never tease Justine about being too organized again.

She held Erica in one arm and checked her temperature with the other.

Two degrees higher than it ought to be. Jennifer carried the baby to the kitchen where she fed her a dose of the medicine.

She offered the baby a bottle, but Erica sucked down barely an ounce before she turned away with a whimper.

Jennifer took the baby to the bathroom to change her diaper. That was when she saw the first of the spots, on Erica's tummy.

This was definitely chicken pox. Jennifer noticed the baby trying to reach them. To keep Erica from scratching, she quickly zipped up the jumper again and wrapped her in a blanket. Erica's brow creased and her mouth puckered, two sure signs that she was about to cry. Jennifer held the baby to her shoulder and began to walk.

"Mary had a little lamb…" she crooned.

Eventually the baby relaxed against Jennifer's chest and her breathing slowed. Since it was a warm evening, Jennifer went outside to the rocking chair on the front porch. As long as she kept up a fairly vigorous rocking motion, Erica seemed satisfied, but the moment she slowed the pace, the baby became restless again.

At least half an hour went by. Erica seemed to be sleeping, but when Jennifer made a move to get up, the baby began to cry. She dropped back to the chair and resumed rocking.

Erica sighed and closed her eyes.

"Oh, Erica. What am I going to do?" In three-and-a-half hours she had to start breakfast, and she was so tired. "Shh, honey, shh. It'll be okay."

At least Jennifer hoped it would. In the morning she would call Justine and if she couldn't reach her, she'd make an appointment with Dr. Marshall. She wanted to make sure she was doing the right things for Erica.

Jennifer hugged the little girl close. She wondered how her own mom had felt on the nights when she'd been sick. Had she worried and felt overwhelmed, too?

It would be nice to be able to talk to her mom about things like that. She'd been gone almost twenty years now, but Jennifer still missed her. She missed Simone, too, and the other forget-me-not friends. Though Harrison and Gabe were still on the island, it wasn't the same.

Erica began to wiggle and Jennifer realized she'd been rocking too slowly. She pushed harder with her exhausted legs, and again the baby settled.

How much longer could she keep this up?

IT WAS VERY LATE, BUT NICK was still awake and writing when he first heard the unfamiliar sound of a baby crying. Half an hour later he heard the crying again, this time out on the porch. He decided to go downstairs to investigate. The front door was open, the screen unlatched. He could hear the creak of the rocker's rails on the wooden porch floor.

He stepped outside into peace and dark. The air seemed to smell even sweeter than it did during the day.

He'd assumed the baby must belong to the new guest in the west room. But it was Jennifer in the rocking chair, holding a sleeping baby against her chest. Though her eyes were closed, she was rocking like a madwoman. In the moonlight, her skin was extremely pale, her eyes shadowed.

She looked exhausted.

And beautiful.

The guilt he'd been trying to deny all day attacked with full force, and as before, he did his best to push it aside. Winning the sympathy and trust of strangers was what he did for a living. How else could he write the books that he did?

So he hadn't told her right away who he was writing about. That was hardly a crime. He'd just wanted her to get to know him as person before he revealed what he was doing.

Yeah. Maybe. But then why did you kiss her?

The plan had been to befriend her, maybe charm her a little. But he drew the line at seduction. At least he had in the past. No wonder she was angry. He was angry at himself.

This book was too important for him to risk it all on one kiss.

The baby stirred in Jennifer's arms and he wondered who she belonged to. In his bare feet, he padded across the wooden floor. He was just a few feet away when Jennifer's eyes flew open and rounded with surprise.

"Nick? What are you doing out here?"

She sounded very alert for someone who had seemed on the verge of sleep a moment ago.

He ignored her question, mostly because he had no answer to give her. It made no sense for him to be here. A smart man would have crawled back to his room and tried to go to sleep.

"Whose baby?"

"This is Justine and Harrison's daughter, Erica."

She glared at him and he caught the subtext in her suddenly accusing eyes. Erica was one of the people Jennifer was worried he would hurt when he published Simone's biography.

"So why are you holding her?"

"I'm babysitting for the night."

"Is she sick?"

Jennifer sighed heavily. "She has the chicken pox and she's probably contagious. Have you had it?"

He nodded. "Does she have a fever?"

"Yes. I've given her medicine for that, but I'm afraid the pox are making her uncomfortable."

"Do you have calamine lotion?"

Her eyes brightened. "I do. I should have thought of that." She rose from the chair, then hesitated when he held out his arms.

"I won't drop her, Jenn."

She passed him the baby, though clearly with some trepidation. She went back inside and barely a minute passed before she returned with the bottle of lotion.

He helped her undress the squirming baby and apply the lotion to the sores. They were mostly on her belly, but the baby had a few on her thighs, as well. When Erica was zipped back into her sleeper, he picked her up again.

"I'll rock her for a while. You get some sleep."

"But she doesn't know you."

He sat and held the baby in the same position he'd observed Jennifer holding her. The baby smelled good and she felt soft and warm against his chest. As soon as he found the right rhythm with the rocker, he felt her relax.

"I guess she likes strangers," he said.

Jennifer was trying hard to look unhappy with the situation, but he could tell, at least he hoped, that she was grateful for the respite.

"Go to bed," he insisted.

"But you're a guest. You shouldn't—"

"I don't mind. Besides, you didn't kick me out so I figure I owe you a favor or two."

"This won't make the other all right."

"I realize that. Now go back to bed. You can't even hold your eyes open anymore."

She sighed and gave him a tiny, reluctant smile. "You're not all bad, Nick Lancaster." Then she backed into the house and he heard her add, "But I almost wish that you were."

JENNIFER DROPPED OFF TO sleep within sixty seconds of putting her head to the pillow. The next thing she knew her radio alarm clicked on and the announcer declared that it was seven in the morning.

Her arm snaked to hit the snooze button, before she remembered.

Erica. Nick.

She sprang out of bed, grabbed a robe and hurried across the hall. Erica was asleep on her back in the cot. Jennifer went closer, brushed a hand over the baby's forehead.

No fever.

She slipped into the bathroom for a quick shower before tackling the breakfast rush. Once she was dressed, she warmed the oven, turned on the coffee and started to cut fruit for blueberry-peach smoothies.

At ten minutes to eight, Nick came into the kitchen. His dark hair was tousled, and he wore the same T-shirt and shorts he'd been in last night. She tried not to stare at his legs, which were so toned that every muscle and tendon stood out in clear relief against his tanned skin.

"You got her to sleep," she said. "Thank you."

His smile felt intimate. "You're welcome."

"How is it you're so good with babies?"

He poured a cup of coffee, then offered it to her. She was about to point out that he was a guest and should serve himself first, but then she decided that that boundary had been crossed so many times she might as well forget about it and accept the coffee. "Thank you."

He poured a second cup for himself. "I once dated a woman who had a child."

"Oh." She was surprised by her instinctive, jealous reaction.

"We were fairly serious, thinking of marriage even. But then the kid's father decided he wanted back in the picture. I was expected to quietly exit stage left. And I did."

He recited the story with calm acceptance, but Jennifer knew that sometimes feelings were not what they seemed on the surface. "That must have been difficult for you."

He shrugged. "Actually the timing was good. My first book was just making the charts and my publishers were anxious for me to deliver something new. So I dived straight into my next project."

And hadn't surfaced since, Jennifer guessed. His answer had her wondering if she'd given him more credit for emotional depth than he deserved.

He surveyed the food spread over the counter. "Can I do something to help?"

He's just trying to win you over. Don't fall for it again.

"Sit down and enjoy your coffee."

He looked at her, amused. "I don't have anything diabolical up my sleeve, Jennifer. Relax." He pulled a knife from the block on the table and started chopping the mushrooms on the cutting board.

She kept working, trying to pretend the situation was normal. But every cell in her body was aware of his physical presence in her kitchen. She was so over her head where Nick Lancaster was concerned. Even now that she knew what he was after, she still found him utterly compelling.

JUSTINE WASN'T ANSWERING her phone when Jennifer called her after breakfast. Erica seemed bright-eyed this morning, with only a slight fever, but still Jennifer knew she'd feel better if she had the baby checked by a professional. She called the clinic in Cedarbrae and was told Dr. Marshall would squeeze her in if she could get there within the hour.

Dr. Marshall was in her late forties or perhaps early fifties and had a calm, reassuring manner.

"This is my third child with chicken pox this week. Fortunately Erica seems to have a mild case of it."

Jennifer told her about the medications she'd administered, the calamine lotion she'd used on the sores. "Was that okay?"

"Absolutely. If Erica's pox continue to trouble her, you may need to put mittens on her hands so she doesn't tear them open. Also, a warm bath with a bit of oatmeal may give her some relief."

"How long will she be contagious?"

"Until the sores have healed over. I'd wait an extra few days after that to be sure."

"Thank you so much, Dr. Marshall." Jennifer did up the snaps of Erica's sleeper, then settled the baby back into her car seat.

The doctor signed off the chart, then placed it on the counter. "And what about you, Jennifer? You look a little tired. I'm guessing you didn't get much sleep last night."

"I'm okay." She flushed, thinking of how helpful Nick had been. Not just last night, but again this morning when she'd been juggling the breakfast routine. He'd fed Erica her bottle while she'd prepared the omelets. Later, he'd helped clear the table so she could make it in time to the clinic.

"Make sure you eat well and get as

much sleep as possible," the doctor advised.

"I'll try." Jennifer left the examining room with a final thank-you. In the waiting room she exchanged sympathetic smiles with two mothers who brought their children to the Sandy Hill Day Care Center. Their children, both toddlers, were playing in the toy center. Apart from the pox marks on their arms and faces, they were acting completely healthy.

On her way out of town, Jennifer drove by Summer Island Realty again, looking for Justine's Lexus. It wasn't there, so she pulled over to use the cell phone. Justine answered, sounding distracted, but cheerful. "Hey, how are you doing? How's Erica?"

"I'm afraid she's come down with the chicken pox."

"Oh, no! Poor baby. And poor you. When did you notice she was sick?"

Jennifer filled her in on the story, including the doctor's calm advice. "So don't worry, Erica's fine. To look at her you'd never guess she wasn't well." Or that she'd been up half the night crying. "We're just on our way back to the B and B now."

"I wish I could jump straight into my car and meet you there, but I need to drop my clients back in Cedarbrae first. Is that all right?"

"No rush," Jennifer assured her, before Justine hung up. She closed her phone and continued driving. As she passed the *Chronicle* office she noticed a battered old Rover parked out front.

Gabe. She'd forgotten all about him. Trust Nick to have had the instinct to interview the one forget-me-not friend she hadn't yet warned about his book.

She paused until the car behind her honked, then reluctantly kept driving. It was too late to do anything about it now.

CHAPTER EIGHT

NICK WAS SITTING IN HIS parked Rover, contemplating his next move, when he saw a tall, fair-headed man carrying a cup of take-out coffee from the bakery to the *Summer Chronicle* office. It was the guy from the ferry.

"Son of a gun." He'd been standing right next to one of the forget-me-not friends and he hadn't even realized it.

Nick jumped out of his vehicle, suddenly in no doubt about what he needed to do next. He traced the other man's path, and entered the historic-looking brick building. Inside, a harried-looking receptionist pointed the way to Gabe Brooke's office.

"Got a minute, Gabe?" she called. "There's someone to see you."

Nick made his own way down the hall and peered inside the open door.

"Sorry about the mess." Gabe removed a stack of paper from a chair and waved him into the seat. His brow furrowed in recognition. "You're the guy from the ferry."

"Nick Lancaster." Gabe showed no reaction, which meant that despite her claim that she'd warned all her friends, Jennifer hadn't gotten to Gabe yet. This might be his one chance for an unbiased interview.

"Name sounds familiar."

"Maybe you've read one of my books?" Nick spotted a familiar cover in the bookshelves behind Gabe's desk. "Looks like you have."

"So you're *that* Nick Lancaster." Gabe sat back in his chair, looking relaxed and intrigued at the same time. "What can I do for you?"

Gabe smiled with an easygoing charm and Nick felt an instant affinity to the guy. He handed him a business card and watched as Gabe glanced at it, then stuck it in his pocket.

"I'm working on a new project," Nick said cautiously. He didn't want to rush the man. Gabe's cooperation would go a long way to adding authenticity to his book. "I'm here to ask your help with my research," he added.

"You want access to past issues of the *Chronicle?* Consider it done."

Nick fumbled with the pen in his hand. "That's great. But I was also hoping to interview you. About Simone DeRosier."

Gabe blinked as he quickly put the facts together. "You're writing a biography about Simone."

"That's right."

"Well." Gabe stared out the window. "In that case, I'll have to thank you for stopping by. I'm sorry I can't help you."

"I wish you would reconsider—"

"Look, I like your work and I'd love to help you. But not with this project. I have nothing to tell you about that woman."

"You sound pretty definitive."

"Simone was an amazing woman, but she wasn't the best thing to ever happen to me. If you're writing her biography, you probably already know that."

Nick conceded the point with a nod. He appreciated the guy's honesty. "Sometimes we need to face the past in order to move on."

"Yeah?" Gabe took a moment to think. "You have a point. Tell you what. If I was going to give you a hand, what would you want from me?"

"Stories. Memories. Observations." Nick took a deep breath. "And photographs if you have them."

"You've got to be kidding. There must be thousands of pictures of that woman in archives around the world. Seemed like she was on a different magazine cover every month."

"I'm not talking about once she was famous. It's pictures of her youth—in particular her teen years—that I'm after."

"In that case, the person you need to talk to is—"

Nick knew who he was going to say before he heard the name.

"Jennifer March," Gabe concluded. "She was always snapping pictures back then."

"Right." Jennifer had a treasure trove on her bulletin board in the kitchen and he'd bet she had a lot more tucked away somewhere. But it didn't seem very likely she'd ever give him permission to use those. "I will ask Jennifer." Again. "But in the meantime, are you sure you don't have anything I could use?"

"I'll look around. But I'm not one for saving much."

Yeah, Nick could tell by the office. Gabe had apologized for the mess, but Nick had never seen a newspaper man with such an organized and sparse working area.

"Pictures aside, I'd really appreciate the opportunity to talk to you about those days. Can I buy you lunch sometime?"

Gabe paused a moment before answering. "I'll think about it, okay?"

"Fair enough." Nick stood. "You have my card. I hope you decide to get in touch. I think Simone would have wanted this book written."

"She loved publicity," Gabe acknowledged. "But since she's no longer alive, her needs aren't really the point anymore, are they?"

GABE SHUT HIS OFFICE DOOR after Nick left. Hell, he hadn't seen that coming at all. What a shock. Nick Lancaster was on Summer Island to write a book about Simone. What a can of worms that man was about to open.

Gabe wished he had a bottle of scotch on the premises. But he hadn't allowed himself to keep any alcohol at work since Nessa left him. He drank too much when he was at home, but he damned well wasn't going to become a drunk at the office, too.

He sat down and his old wooden chair creaked and groaned as it took his weight. Jenna, who handled the receptionist position here, as well as about ten other jobs, was after him to buy one of those ergonomic, fabric-covered chairs, the kind with adjustable settings. She said it would be good for his back. But Gabe couldn't imagine ever parting with the worn maple chair that had been used by his father and his grandfather before him.

He closed his eyes as an old sadness settled like an ache between his shoulder blades. Three generations of Brookes had lived on Summer Island. They'd run the local real estate office and newspaper and sat on the Island Trust.

But he was the end of the line.

When he and Nessa had been married he'd assumed that one day they would have a child. He hadn't particularly worried when year after year passed with nothing happening.

They were young. Still in their thirties. They had plenty of time.

Of course, for a good many of those years, he'd been preoccupied by Simone. Theirs had been a demanding, exciting sort of friendship. With the benefit of hindsight, he thought that he'd probably given a great deal more than he'd ever gotten in return.

Especially if you factored in the breakup of his marriage.

Nessa had been a good wife, the best, really. And she'd loved him. She had really loved him. But he'd frittered away that love by treating her like she was expendable.

When she'd told him she was leaving him, he hadn't believed her at first.

Then he'd found out about the multiple sclerosis and for the first time in his life he'd been scared to death. Nessa didn't deserve that. Nobody did… Unless it was him.

But it hadn't been. If he was thankful for one thing, it was that Nessa didn't seem to have been afflicted with a progressive form of the disease.

Gabe grabbed a piece of paper from the in-box on the corner of his desk. He stared at it, trying to focus. It had been months since he'd allowed himself to indulge all his old regrets.

He couldn't relapse now. Nessa had built herself a new life. It was time for him to do the same.

The problem was, he didn't have a clue where to start.

His BlackBerry beeped, reminding him of his one o'clock appointment with Molly Springfield at the realty office. He checked the time, then the stack of articles he had yet to edit. Looked like this was going to be a working lunch.

JUSTINE ARRIVED AT THE B and B just fifteen minutes after Jennifer got home from the doctor's appointment.

"I'm so sorry, Jenn." Justine held out her arms and Erica went to her with a half whimper, half smile. "Did you get any sleep last night?"

"Erica was a little unsettled," Jennifer admitted. "But she's been great this morning." After the appointment, she'd played happily in the office while Jennifer had checked the Internet for Nick's books. She'd been pretty impressed to see the caliber of work he produced and had ended up ordering one of his books from Amazon.

"I really owe you after this, Jenn. I hope no one else gets sick. Have your dad and aunt had the chicken pox?"

"Yes. No problem there. But Dr. Marshall says Erica will be contagious until all the sores have healed over, so you may be housebound for a week or more."

Justine thanked her again, then gathered all her baby paraphernalia and headed home. By then it was too late for Jennifer to make her usual yoga class. She waited until it was over, then called Molly.

"Sorry I missed class today. I was baby-sitting Erica for Justine. Any chance you could pop over this afternoon for tea?"

"I'd love to Jenn, but I'm just on my way out the door for an appointment. How was your afternoon with that guy yesterday?"

"Nick Lancaster? It was fun until I found out why he's here."

"Oh?"

"It turns out he's on Summer Island to research a biography about Simone. And he booked into Lavender Farm because he knew I was one of the forget-me-not friends."

There was a pause. "Really?"

"Yeah." Jennifer closed her eyes and rubbed her forehead. "We talked for hours before he told me this. I wanted to kick him out, but for some reason Dad has really taken to him and he won't hear of it."

"Too bad. He sounds like a real jerk."

Jennifer wanted to agree, but she couldn't. She didn't like the way Nick had handled the whole biography thing, but he'd been nice in other ways.

Or had he? She still wasn't sure how to interpret the helpful things he'd done since his arrival. Was he at heart a kind, decent person? Or were his good deeds merely calculated moves to earn her trust?

"I told him he could stay on Summer Island if he wanted, but I wasn't going to help with his book. I've already warned Justine, too, and she's going to talk to Harrison and Nessa."

"Good for you."

"I forgot to phone Gabe, though. I noticed Nick's SUV by the *Chronicle*'s office this morning, so I think he got to him before I did."

"Nick's spoken to Gabe?" Molly sounded truly alarmed.

"Don't worry. I doubt if Gabe would have been very helpful. Maybe if enough people stonewall him, Nick will go back to New York and forget about this book."

"I don't think Nick Lancaster is the kind of man who gives up easily."

Jennifer frowned. How would Molly know? Before she could say anything, Molly was talking again.

"I mean he doesn't *sound* like that kind of guy."

"I'm afraid you're right about that. Oh, Moll, what am I going to do? Why did this happen just when things were going so well for everybody?"

"You mean Harrison and Nessa?"

"Yes. They're both in good relationships, finally, and Harrison and Justine have the new baby. Autumn is really thriving these days, too."

"What about your other forget-me-not friend?" Molly asked softly.

"Aidan? He and Rae are in corporate heaven from what I hear. Their son turned one just last week. I sent him the cutest pair of overalls for a present."

"I wasn't referring to Aidan."

Jennifer rubbed her forehead again. "You mean Gabe."

"Yes."

"Well, you're right. He isn't doing that great. Say, have you given any thought to my idea? I could invite you both for dinner on Saturday. Gabe's got to be the most eligible man on the island. Think you might be interested?"

It took so long for Molly to answer that Jennifer worried she'd offended her. She was about to apologize, when Molly finally replied.

"Actually, that's not a bad suggestion, except for one thing."

"Oh?"

"I'm thinking I may need to sell my cottage and move off the island."

CHAPTER NINE

MOLLY MADE UP AN EXCUSE about financial difficulties and business matters to take care of in Toronto. As a friend Jennifer deserved better, but over the past three years Molly had become so used to hiding information about herself, that she did it quite naturally.

That couldn't be a good thing.

Molly disconnected the call, after assuring Jenn they'd have lunch together soon to discuss the move. She grabbed her purse and ran out to the car, anxious not to be late for her meeting with Gabe.

Perhaps it was just as well that Nick had come to the island and forced her hand. She didn't want to live her life this way, hiding her true identity and motivations from the people who meant the most to her.

Maybe if I just came clean now...

But she'd been deceiving everyone for too long. They'd never forgive her. And she didn't have the right to ask them to.

If only she'd stuck to her original plan, she wouldn't be in this mess. It had only taken a month, after all, to learn all she'd needed about Simone and to make sure Autumn was all right.

With each mile that passed as Molly zipped along the ocean-front road, she felt increasingly confident that she was making the right decision.

She parked in front of the realty office, then made her way inside.

"Hi, Flora. How's your husband?"

"Lots of trouble, like usual." Flora frowned at her. "You were supposed to be here at one o'clock."

Molly glanced at her watch. She was two minutes late. "Yes, I—"

"Molly! Good to see you." Gabe strode past the receptionist's desk and ushered her inside. "Come into my office and we'll have a chat."

Curious for clues about him, she glanced around. Though the real estate business had been in the Brooke family for three generations now, Gabe's office was neither big nor showy. A picture of Gabe's father seated in the same chair that Gabe now occupied, proved that it had been over a decade since the last remodel.

His chair squeaked as Gabe leaned toward her. "I've been thinking about what you said at the bakery. I'm not sure trading up would be in your best interests right now. You might find you'd lose more business than you expect when you change your location. Besides, you've spent years fixing up the old Wythe cottage. You wouldn't want to start from scratch with a new place would you?"

"I wasn't planning to trade up, Gabe. I'm moving. I need to leave Summer Island."

He frowned as if thinking he hadn't heard her correctly. "But why?"

She stared out the window. Lying to Gabe in person was much more difficult than fudging the truth to Jennifer over the phone. "It's just not working out for me here the way I'd hoped. I want to put the cottage on the market. Once it's sold I'll be moving back to Toronto."

"Oh." Gabe sank back into his seat. He glanced away from her, rubbed his jaw thoughtfully, then focused back on her. "You're sure you want to do this?"

She nodded and he reached for the bottom drawer of his desk. It stuck and he had to give a harder tug. "Okay, let's do up a contract. I know the cottage well, so I can tell you right away what I think you should ask for it." He scribbled a number on a piece of paper and handed it to her.

It was a hundred thousand more than she'd paid. "That much?"

"Real estate has gone up a lot in the past few years."

Molly placed the paper back on his desk. That was when she saw the business card. It was Nick Lancaster's. She couldn't help herself—she picked it up. "Have you been talking to this man?"

"He came to the newspaper office to see me this morning. Do you know him?"

"He picked up Jennifer after her yoga class yesterday. She was planning to show him around the island."

"That surprises me. I wouldn't have thought she'd want anything to do with the man who was writing a biography about Simone."

"You're right about that. She didn't find out what he was up to until later. When she did, she called Justine and Nessa and warned them not to talk to him."

"Good. I admire Lancaster as a writer, but I sure wish he was here to work on a different project. He's just going to dredge up the past, when what we need, all of us who were close to Simone, is to get on with the future."

"Your ex-wife has certainly done that." As far as Molly could tell though, Gabe had not. Whenever she saw him around town he was always alone.

Gabe looked annoyed. Then suddenly he laughed. "You tell it like it is, don't you Molly?"

"So I've been told."

"Well, you're right. Yes, my ex-wife has made a new life for herself. And I'm glad. Nessa deserves to be happy. Last thing I want is Nick Lancaster opening old wounds for her."

"It's nice of you to be so concerned about your ex. But what about you? Have you moved on, too?" She was being bold, Molly knew. But at this point, what did she have to lose? Gabe obviously needed *someone* to give him a prod.

Gabe viewed her speculatively. "Molly, would you like to go out to dinner Friday night?"

If only he'd asked her this six months ago.

"Molly?"

"But—I'm moving."

He smiled. "Not until your house sells, right?"

"Right." He'd asked her to dinner. Not for a long-term relationship.

"So…dinner at eight at the Owl's Nest? How does that sound?"

Only the nicest restaurant on the island. Suddenly she felt a little dizzy. She'd come in here to sell her house and had ended up with a date, as well. How ironic that it wasn't until she decided to move that Gabe had shown any interest in her.

Wasn't that just like a man?

HIS CONVERSATION WITH GABE Brooke had not gone well, but Nick wasn't discouraged. He hadn't expected instant success. Simone's friends were a loyal bunch. He'd known that before he'd set out on the cross-country drive from New York. All he could hope was that he'd set the stage. He knew he'd be talking to Gabe again.

Nick had walked the two blocks from the *Chronicle* office to the local library. The small brick building had an inviting air about it, enhanced by two crumbling terra-cotta planters that flanked the main door and overflowed with blue and pink flowers. Two wrought iron benches sat on either side of the planters.

He inhaled the odor of moldy old books as he stepped inside. A young woman, dressed so stereotypically as a librarian that he almost laughed, glanced up at him. The sign on her desk said her name was Emma Parks, and she couldn't have been anywhere close to the age of thirty, yet she wore thick dark glasses, her hair in a bun, and a cardigan that was at least two sizes too large.

"You're new," she said. Then blushed and glanced down at her desk.

"I'm Nick Lancaster. I'm visiting the island to do some research for a book."

The color in her face deepened. "I've read your books. And I saw you on *Larry King*. What are you writing about this time?"

"Simone DeRosier. A biography."

"Oh, of course. I should have guessed."

He saw no censure in her eyes and guessed that Emma Parks was too young to have any stake in what the biography might expose. "I'd like to review any articles about Simone in the local paper. Do you keep past issues on microfiche?"

"Not yet," Emma confessed, sounding embarrassed that her town was so behind the times. "But you're welcome to go through the actual newspapers. I'll show you where we keep them."

She led him to a back room and pointed out a table where he could work. Now Nick was in his element and he found he enjoyed the physical pleasure of reading from the old, yellowed newsprint.

Over the years, plenty of articles had featured the island's most famous summer resident. They were mostly human interest stories, but they would be very useful in helping him round out his understanding of the artist.

"You're working hard," Emma commented a few hours later, as she passed by his table pushing a trolley cart loaded with books.

"So are you." He'd noticed her occasionally through the open door, answering calls, helping customers, re-shelving books.

"I was just about to stop for a coffee break. Can I get you a cup?"

"Sure, that would be great. Just black for me."

A few minutes later she returned with two mugs. Hers was almost white she'd added so much cream.

"So how long have you lived on the island?" he asked.

"All my life," she replied, predictably. "Though I went to university in Victoria." She shook her head. "I don't know how people live in those big cities."

If she'd been overwhelmed by Victoria, he wondered how she'd feel about New York.

"Did you know Simone?" He thought she was too young, but you never knew.

To his surprise Emma nodded. "I used to babysit her daughter Autumn. Such a sweet girl."

Nick grinned as he reached for his pen and paper. Sometimes, you just got lucky.

AFTER HE'D FINISHED AT THE library, Nick climbed into his Rover intending to make it to the B and B in time for tea. Halfway there, he spotted something on the road ahead. Not another vehicle...it wasn't moving. He kept driving, but slowed his speed until he was finally close enough to see what was in his way.

It was a cow. A big black cow with horns and a baleful expression.

Nick scoped out the surrounding fields. A herd of cattle were grazing in the pasture to the right. There was a hole in the fence, which explained why this animal was running free. He thought for a minute, then laid on the horn.

The cow simply stared at him.

Nick laughed, then reached for his camera. Stepping out of the car, he framed a picture, then took it. He shot several before he was finally close enough to the animal that it started to back off.

"Hey, buddy, you're actually kind of beautiful." He watched the animal lope off the road, toward the pasture, and his amusement faded into wonder.

He was a big city person and had always preferred the company of people to animals. But there was something about that cow, and these hills, and this island that got to him. He climbed back into the vehicle and drove the rest of the way to the B and B.

Out of everything he'd seen on Summer Island so far, this farm was one of the prettiest spots. Rolling hills, an ocean view and the lavender, of course. He didn't know a lot about farming, but he estimated over an acre of land had been planted in the tall spiky plants, covered in blossoms that ranged from pale blue to deep purple.

Nick's eyes narrowed as he noticed a figure near the southern border of the property. He removed his sunglasses, tossed them on the dash of the Rover, then set out in pursuit.

He could tell that Jennifer had seen him. She kept her back to him as he approached, but he saw her stiffen, as if she were preparing herself for a confrontation.

If she knew how free the local librarian had been with her information about the personal side of Simone DeRosier, she'd probably be even more prickly. That was the last thing he wanted. He searched for a neutral topic.

"Where's the baby?" he asked, when he was only a few feet away.

Jennifer turned to acknowledge him. "Justine picked her up before lunch." She swallowed. "Thanks again for coming to our rescue."

"No problem. She's cute."

"You like babies?"

"Sure." He'd always wanted kids one day. Karen's son had been a year old when he'd first moved in with them. After the relationship ended, he'd missed that baby more than the mother. For several months, he hadn't dated anyone. Just in case Karen changed her mind and decided she wanted him back.

She never had.

His friends had told him to count his blessings. "Why would you want to raise another man's child? You've got your freedom again. Enjoy it."

And in the end, that's exactly what he'd done. What he was still doing.

He fingered a stalk of the lavender. "These are a darker color than the ones by the house."

"These are English cultivars. I grow mostly French varieties near the house. The Alba are almost pure white and the Super are the best for extracting essential oils."

She'd lost a little of her wariness. He took a step forward. Her shoulders were smooth, lightly tanned, and taunted him from beneath her sleeveless dress. "How many different varieties do you grow?"

"At least a dozen, though I'd like to add more." She crouched to snip off another bunch and added the stalks to her basket. "I use this Irene Doyle cultivar to make ice cream."

He noticed the scent was particularly powerful in this part of the garden. Or was it Jennifer's perfume that filled his senses? Interestingly enough, she didn't smell like lavender. Her scent was something a little more like lemon, refreshing and citrusy.

"Lavender ice cream?" he asked, just to keep her talking. "I can't imagine that would taste very good."

"The flavor is subtle. You infuse scalding cream and sugar with dried lavender, before adding the eggs."

Her voice was calm, but he could tell she was unsettled. She kept licking her bottom lip. Not the top one, just the bottom.

He wanted to touch her. He didn't know why, but the impulse annoyed him. He was here to earn Jennifer's trust. To get her help and her permission to use those photographs.

He had to remember that. Still, when he was around her something sweet and slightly mystical happened to him. He had an almost overwhelming urge to pull her into his arms and carry her off.

"Nick. Don't look at me like that." She took several steps backward, stumbling a little on the uneven ground.

He held up his hands to show her he was harmless. "I'm not going to try anything. I promise."

"It's just that I can't…"

"What? Fraternize with the enemy?" He noticed that her basket was empty. All the lavender had scattered to the ground. He bent and did his best to gather whatever he could.

"Thanks," she said, not meeting his eyes.

"Can we talk? Just for a minute?"

"I suppose."

He set her basket on a large stepping-stone then reached for her hand. Reluctantly, she let him lead her to a bench under a nearby arbutus tree.

"Jennifer, I understand that you have a strong loyalty to Simone. She was a very close friend. I get that. But why are you so opposed to this biography?"

What do you have to hide?

It had to be something, didn't it?

"I want to remember the good things about my friend. Is that so wrong? Anyway, why are you so determined to write this book? Simone was just an entertainer. You—you've written about *presidents*."

So she'd checked him out. And her question was a fair one. He'd give her as honest an answer as he could. "The truth is, I can't explain why some subjects excite me and others don't. At first, it was Simone's death that intrigued me. I wanted to understand why someone with so much to live for would commit suicide. Then, when we found out she'd been murdered, I found myself wondering how one woman had become the focal point of so much obsession. Not just in her public life, but her private life, too."

"Simone always loved to be loved."

Did Jennifer realize her voice contained

a hint of bitterness when she said that? Nick doubted that she did.

"Why do you think she was that way? Do you think it had something to do with her mother?" Simone's mother had deserted the family when Simone was eleven years old. So far Nick had not been able to locate Andrea DeRosier to find out why. But before he'd left for the island, he'd hired an investigator to work on the mystery.

"Probably. Simone never stopped hoping she would one day see her again."

"And did she?"

"Sadly, no." Jennifer rolled her eyes. "Now, I'm helping you, aren't I? Answering your questions when I promised I wouldn't."

"Promised who?"

"Mainly myself."

She looked so miserable that he couldn't help but feel a little sorry for her. "Jennifer, you're not betraying Simone's memory by talking to me. Don't you think she would have wanted this book to be written? To be finally understood for the person she really was?"

"You're right about one thing. Simone did love publicity. She used to flip through my copies of *People* and *Us* and point out the pictures of herself."

"Didn't you get tired of that?"

"It was fun," she assured him. "Simone craved the limelight as much as I hated it. We were so different in that way."

"That's probably what made it possible for you to be such close friends."

"You're right. Simone never saw me as competition the way she saw other women."

"And you didn't resent that?"

"Why would I resent her for having something I didn't even want?"

He thought he had her now. "So then you admit that Simone would approve of me writing this book?"

"No. Simone loved attention, but not at the expense of her daughter. This book will only open old wounds."

"What wounds are you talking about?

The relationship between Simone and Gabe? It's common knowledge, Jennifer. I won't be dwelling on it, I assure you of that."

"It will still be painful for Nessa," she insisted. "Besides, there are others to protect. Like Autumn."

"I don't understand how this book will hurt her. Jennifer, I think the person you're really worried about is yourself."

She pulled away. "That's ridiculous."

If it was, then why was she reacting so strongly? What were this woman's secrets? Nick wanted to know. Badly.

"Talk to me, Jenn. It might be good for you to face your demons."

"*You're* my demon, Nick." She pushed off the bench and started walking away from him. "And I meant what I said. No matter how nice you are to me and my family, I'm not going to help you with this book."

CHAPTER TEN

THE NEXT AFTERNOON, AIDAN called Jennifer from Seattle.

"I hear trouble's afoot," he said.

Jennifer perched on the kitchen stool. "You mean Nick Lancaster."

"Yeah. Justine says you're pretty concerned about the biography he's writing. Has the guy been hounding you to death?"

"Pretty much." She thought of their conversation yesterday in the garden. She'd been so angry with him, yet that hadn't stopped her from remembering the time he'd kissed her...and wishing it could happen again. "He's staying here, at the B and B. His agent booked him in for a month before we knew what he was up to."

"Shoot. And you can't kick him out?"

"I wanted to, but Dad won't hear of it. Nick fixed a leaking toilet practically the first day he was here. Plus he's a history buff like Dad."

"Ingratiating himself with the host. Smart."

"Yes. And usually Dad's such a good judge of character…" She sighed. "When are you coming to the island next? We need to sit down and strategize on how to contain this situation."

Aidan laughed.

"I'm serious. This book could mess up everything."

"Sorry, Jenn. I didn't mean to make light of the problem. And that's why I was calling. To let you know that Rae and I will be driving to Summer Island with Harrison tomorrow."

"Will you be bringing Layton?"

"Sure will. We were hoping the gang could meet at Pebble Beach tomorrow night after dark. Harrison's already called Nessa and Dex and they've agreed to come, too."

"What about Gabe?"

Aidan hesitated.

"We need to be united in our approach to this, Aidan."

"You're right. I guess I'd better invite him, as well. Harrison's going to have a cow but he'll have to deal with it."

Yes, he would. Jennifer hung up the phone feeling much less stressed than she had before the call. Her friends were coming to the rescue. It was nice to know that after all these years she could still count on them.

AFTER HER TALK WITH AIDAN, Jennifer headed to Cedarbrae for a few supplies. Her thoughts were busy as she drove, but that didn't stop her from noticing the For Sale sign situated prominently on Molly's front lawn.

"What in the world?" She checked the rearview mirror to make sure no one was following her closely, then braked hard and pulled a U-turn. She parked on the edge of the road and ran across to Molly's front door. A moment after she pressed the doorbell, the curtains parted, then Molly stepped out. She had on a pretty floral dress and strappy sandals.

"Wait," she said before Jennifer could say a word. "Let's sit down so we can talk. For the record, I've been meaning to pop over but I've been so busy. I didn't want to tell you over the phone."

"This is happening awfully fast, Molly. I don't understand." She glanced again at the For Sale sign and saw Gabe's name and number listed on the bottom.

Molly dragged Jennifer to a couple of chairs under a cedar tree and Jennifer sat down reluctantly.

"I told you I was going to move, Jenn. I'm going back to Toronto."

"But it was just a few days ago that you said you might need to move." She'd mentioned financial difficulties. But that had come so out of the blue. Molly had never given any sign of being short of money before. "If you're having trouble making payments, maybe I can help."

"Jenn, you're so kind. It's just—" Molly glanced out toward the ocean. She ran her fingers through her unruly curls. "Something came up. I wasn't expecting it and now I've got to go home."

"But I thought Summer Island *was* your home now." After all, she didn't have any family still living to tie her to the city where she'd been born and raised.

Was something other than family pulling her? Lately, she and Molly had both been complaining about the scarcity of eligible men their age. Maybe Molly had an old boyfriend waiting for her in Ontario. "Is this about a guy?"

Molly looked relieved that she'd guessed it. "Yes."

"Is he a good guy? Do you care about him?"

Molly nodded and Jennifer tried to feel glad for her. But this didn't feel right. "You never mentioned there was someone."

"I thought we were finished. I didn't expect to ever see him again."

Jennifer waited, but Molly didn't offer

more. "So…what's he like? Are you excited? When did he get in touch with you?"

Molly held up her hands and laughed. "We were…in touch…at the beginning of the week. Sorry I can't tell you much more. It's all been kind of crazy."

"Do you have a picture?"

"No, and I'm afraid I really don't have time to talk right now. I'm going out for dinner with Gabe. He'll be picking me up any minute."

"Gabe?" Another big surprise. "But what about the other guy?"

"It isn't a date. We're talking business." Molly pointed at the For Sale sign.

"Okay. Sure." But if the dinner wasn't a date, why was Molly all dressed up?

Molly stood, obliging Jennifer to do the same. She walked her across the street to the old pickup.

"I'm sorry, Jennifer."

She was still trying to absorb everything. Molly was moving. She couldn't believe it. "I'm going to miss you."

Molly blinked, then looked away. "I'll miss you, too."

"What about the yoga studio?"

"I'll have to close it."

This couldn't be happening. Molly had put so much into decorating the cottage and starting her business. Why would she walk away from all of that for a guy that she'd never even talked about before?

"Molly—"

At the sound of an approaching car, Molly had to step off the road. "I'll call you," she said, as Gabe's sports car pulled up in front of her house.

Reluctantly Jennifer nodded. She waved at Gabe, who was eyeing her curiously, then took off for Pebble Beach. Her errands could wait until another day.

FIVE MINUTES LATER, JENNIFER nosed the pickup into a parking spot that faced the ocean. She kicked her sandals off then went out to sit on the warm hood, her bare feet dangling.

It was growing dark and the water shimmered with the colors of harvest fruit, plum, peach, raspberry and apricot. It was a beautiful sunset. Jennifer stared at the familiar scene but her thoughts were on other places. She couldn't get the image of that For Sale sign out of her head.

For Molly's sake, she hoped this was something good. That the guy was great and that the move would be something that would make Molly happy.

But she was going to miss her…

Jennifer hopped off the truck and started to walk. Everything in her life seemed so topsy-turvy lately, starting with Nick Lancaster's arrival.

Nick. Yesterday she'd called him her demon. But he was more like a ghost, haunting her, always there in her thoughts, no matter what she said or did or where she went.

She felt drawn to him and the pull was almost as strong as her opposition to the book he was writing. Her stomach knotted and ached just thinking about it.

Simone was dead. Why couldn't that

be the end of it? Why did everyone need to probe and examine and explain and prod? Jennifer just wanted to be left in peace.

But Nick wasn't going to do that.

She felt it in her bones.

It was as if he could see right through her. Through her to something that she hadn't even known she had inside her.

Jennifer kicked a piece of driftwood out of her path. She didn't like where her thoughts were taking her. She couldn't let Nick do this to her.

Remember the good times you had with Simone. The shopping expeditions. The fun and extravagant presents. The late nights spent laughing and talking.

Jennifer waded into the ocean until the water lapped to the edge of her skirt. As the waves pulled back, she felt the sand disappear from under her toes. That's what Nick Lancaster did to her, too. He was eroding the foundation of her life and he didn't even seem to comprehend the damage he was doing.

She started walking again, letting the waves pull her a little this way, a little that. Slowly she headed for the boardwalk that led to town. Just as she'd reached it, another vehicle pulled into the parking lot next to her truck. In the near dark all she could see was a pair of headlights, then the silhouette of a man as he stepped out from the driver's side.

Nick. She knew the shape of him by now.

What was he doing here?

She waited while he scrambled down the hill to join her. No sense pretending she didn't know who he was or that he'd come here to talk to her. Suddenly she felt as if her blood had been replaced with champagne. All giddy and unsettled. Why did he have this effect on her when he had the power to make her life so miserable, too?

It didn't make sense and yet she couldn't change the way she felt. As he drew closer, she could see that his gaze was fixed on her. Not once did he break eye contact. When they were within speaking distance he said, "You okay?"

She shrugged. There was no way to answer that question. She was and she wasn't. In one way she felt more alive than she could ever remember. And yet at the same time she was also more exposed. Nick had the power to hurt her with more than his pen.

And he knew it.

"May I join you?"

She didn't answer, just continued in the direction she'd been taking earlier. He fell in beside her.

Though a foot separated them, she could feel his warmth, smell the clean male scent of him, salty and fresh like the ocean. They didn't talk as they strolled along the shore until they came to a spot Jennifer remembered well.

"We used to have our bonfires here."

"Nice." Nick settled on one of the logs that faced the blackened circle bordered with rocks. She hesitated, then sat next to him, leaving a good space between them.

"This is where the forget-me-not gang used to hang out, isn't it?"

She tensed, despite having anticipated that he would ask about that. This was common knowledge after all. Nothing to be secretive about.

And anyway, she wanted to talk about this. The happy stuff. The good old days. "Gabe would smuggle beer from his father's supply. We'd talk and roast hotdogs. Those boys were always hungry."

He laughed softly. "I remember my mother complaining about the same thing when I was that age."

"What's she like, your mother?"

"An ex-English teacher. Books are her specialty. When it came to the practical stuff of running a household and a car and using the computer, she pretty much relied on me."

He spoke affectionately, so Jennifer knew he didn't really mind.

"Her new husband does all that for her now," he said, stretching out his legs, almost as if there were a fire in front of them that offered warmth.

"Do you miss looking after your mom?"

"You know, I haven't really thought about it, but I think you're right. I do a little."

Maybe he liked looking after people more than he knew. Despite his claim of being a loner focused on work, he'd gravitated to a care-giving role from the moment he'd checked into their B and B.

So maybe his kindness wasn't all an act. At least not one hundred percent an act.

Jennifer felt something tickle her leg. She looked down to see a spider scurrying across her ankle. "Oh!" She brushed it off, then immediately felt guilty. "I hope I didn't kill it."

"What was it?"

"A spider. Simone used to get so mad at us if we killed one." She went quiet, realizing she'd opened the one subject she'd wanted to avoid.

Of course, Nick wasn't going to ignore this opportunity.

"A few people have told me she liked spiders," he said. "Unusual for a girl, isn't it?"

"Her mother read her *Charlotte's Web* when she was little. Simone loved that story. Took it to heart."

"I remember it. The spider dies after she gives birth, right?"

Jennifer had never made that connection before, but she realized he was probably right. Simone would have identified with that.

"It was right here, on this spot, that you first met Simone, wasn't it?"

She nodded.

"I wonder what that was like for you. For years you'd been the only girl in the group. And suddenly there was Simone. Simone who always had to be the center of attention wherever she went."

"I didn't mind. I was glad not to be the only girl anymore. You have to remember I grew up with those guys. I wasn't interested in them that way."

Thinking of Gabe, and her long-ago

crush, she had to look away. She picked up an old stick and prodded the dead ashes, aware that Nick was watching her closely.

"Why is it so hard for you to admit to feeling jealous of Simone?"

"I wasn't jealous." Well, maybe just a little. After all, Harrison had been the most attentive boyfriend any girl could ask for. Why had Simone found it so necessary to string Gabe along, too?

But there was no point blaming Simone for that. Even if she hadn't encouraged Gabe, that didn't mean Gabe ever would have noticed Jennifer. At least not in *that* way.

"Whatever you say, Jenn."

His stubborn refusal to believe her was maddening. "Sorry to disappoint you, Nick. Were you hoping to add a little soap opera drama to your book?"

"This isn't about my book. In case you haven't noticed, I wasn't talking about Simone just now. I was talking about you. Don't you think it's time you knocked your friend off that pedestal you've placed her on? Or at least admitted to yourself that you've put her up there?"

She didn't dare respond to that. "I wonder how you would you like it if I put your life under the microscope the way you keep doing to me."

"Be my guest. What would you like to know?"

She was surprised by the offer. Then intrigued. She had so many questions. One in particular... "The woman you almost married, the one with the child, what happened there, Nick? Why didn't you stick it out with her?"

"You want to get into that? Fine. I'll tell you. Her ex came back from some job he was doing in South America. He wanted to be part of the kid's life again. Hell, he wanted to be part of Karen's life, too. I wasn't going to stand in the way."

Honorable. If it was true. "So that's when you decided to focus one hundred percent on your writing career."

"Would you have admired me more if I'd chosen to die of a broken heart?"

Jennifer studied his face, the intense expression, the challenging set to his mouth. Did he care if she admired him or not? Probably not.

She had to remember that this conversation—like every other conversation she'd had with him—was just another tactic to try and win her trust, and therefore her cooperation.

"Come on, Nick. You don't care what I think."

"Is that a fact? You seem pretty sure of yourself, Jenn. I wonder if the world might be a little more complicated than you're willing to admit."

"Well, *you're* certainly more complicated than I guessed when I first met you. At least more manipulative and secretive."

"Wow, another jab. Isn't it getting a little old? Or are you going to keep blaming me for that forever?"

If she hadn't known better, she would have sworn he was being sincere. That he really did care what she thought. And, therefore, that she might mean more to him than another reference source for his book.

But she did know better. And she wasn't going to back down an inch. "I'll keep blaming you until you change your mind about this book."

He let out a long, exasperated sigh.

Jennifer got to her feet and brushed the sand off the back of her skirt. She wondered what Nick would say if he knew that in less than twenty-four hours she'd be meeting her friends in this very spot to plot against him.

She had a feeling he wouldn't be surprised.

CHAPTER ELEVEN

IT WAS PAST MIDNIGHT WHEN Jennifer arrived home with Nick right behind her. He said good night then went up to his room. She knew she wouldn't sleep, so she went into the kitchen and mixed eggs, milk and vanilla into a big bowl. She lined a casserole dish with stale bread, then poured the egg mixture over top. In the morning she'd bake this and cook some chicken-apple sausage to go with it.

She ground the coffee and filled the canister with water.

As she performed the usual, comforting tasks, she was able to keep her mind from straying. But as soon as she was in bed, Nick was all she could think about.

She replayed every moment of their

evening together. Pictured him, alone, in the queen-size bed upstairs. Tossed and turned and wondered what might have happened if they'd met under different circumstances.

Sometimes when he looked at her, she felt exposed in a way she'd never been before. It wasn't a bad feeling. In a way it was kind of…exciting. She was used to fading into the background. Too bad Nick's flattering attention had more to do with her knowledge of Simone than her own personality.

Sleep, Jennifer, she commanded herself.

And finally she did.

NICK DID NOT SLEEP WELL that night. He kept thinking about Jennifer and seeing her hunted expression as he'd tried to figure her out. The thing he couldn't understand was why it mattered to him so much, why he cared whether Jennifer harbored hidden resentment toward Simone or not.

As he'd said to her, this wasn't material

he could use in his book. Clearly, he was getting distracted.

Jennifer was an important research source for him. She wasn't supposed to interest him in any other way. Likewise, her opinion about him shouldn't matter one way or the other.

Yet he hated the way Jennifer made him feel like a scum-feeding tabloid reporter. He wasn't. He was a responsible journalist, with three respectable titles to his résumé. And this one would be no less good, he'd make damn sure of that.

At dawn, he gave up on his restless night and powered up his laptop for a couple of hours of work. At eight he went for breakfast, where Jennifer did an expert job of avoiding him. He helped Annie and Phil with the dishes, despite their repeated protests, then headed to Cedarbrae and the local real estate office.

Summer Island Reality was in another historic looking building, this one made of stone. He pushed through the glass-fronted door and encountered a stocky, dark-haired matron.

"You have an appointment?"

He pegged the accent as Greek, which matched with the olive-toned skin and the almond-colored eyes. "Actually no. I was hoping to see Justine Kincaid, if she's in. I understand her baby, Erica, has been ill."

It was the right thing to say. The woman's distrustful attitude vanished immediately, as she assumed that if he knew about Justine's baby, he must be a close friend.

"Yes, she's here. She just stopped by to pick up her messages. She'll be working from home until Erica is better. Thank goodness Harrison is coming back today."

Harrison was on his way back to Summer Island? Nick mentally filed this important information as he followed the woman to an office.

"Someone to see you, Justine. Want me to hold the baby?"

Inside, Nick beheld a scene of moderate chaos. Papers were strewn everywhere.

Justine was trying to jot down notes from her answering machine, while she jostled an unhappy Erica on one knee.

Before Justine could respond, the woman had whisked the baby away and closed the door behind Nick.

"Hi, Justine. I'm Nick Lancaster."

Justine ran her hands through her tousled hair. At first she looked ambushed. The next moment, amused.

"So, you've got me cornered, Nick Lancaster. I'm impressed. Usually Flora is more difficult to win over than that."

"I got past her defenses by mentioning your baby. It turns out I'm on closer acquaintance with your daughter than with you."

"Oh?"

"I spelled Jennifer for a shift the other night so she could get some sleep."

A look of guilt shadowed Justine's friendly face. "That was rotten of me, wasn't it? Dropping off a sick baby…"

"You didn't know she was coming down with the chicken pox. And Erica was very good once I finally figured out the right rhythm on the rocking chair."

Justine laughed, then looked at him with something like regret. "You seem like a very nice man. It's too bad I have to ask you to go away."

"Why would you do that? I assure you, I'm a respectable journalist. I'm not out to write trash."

"I'm afraid the truth will give you more than enough room to write something quite sensationalist. Take all those men Simone paraded to her various celebrity functions even though she was a married woman. Then there was the manner of her death… murder is the ultimate in sensationalism, isn't it?"

Justine began organizing the piles of paper on her desk. "But all of that is public knowledge. You must have come here looking for something else. I wonder what that might be?"

"I'm not making a secret of it," he said. "One of the things I'd like to work out is who she wrote that song for."

"The forget-me-not song?"

"Exactly."

"Good luck with that. She told every one of her friends, as well as her husband, that she'd written it for them. God only knows who she really had in mind when she wrote it."

Maybe. But Nick still held out hope that someone on earth might, too.

"Listen, Nick—"

"Please, just one more question. Do you know anything about Simone's mother?"

Justine went still. "You really go for the jugular, don't you? Harrison has always wondered about her. Simone wouldn't allow him to hire an investigator. Have you found out anything? Have you managed to track her down?"

"Not yet," he had to admit. "I'm working on that angle, but I'd hoped your husband would have some of the answers I need."

"If he did, I doubt that he would tell you."

"Yeah, you're probably right."

Justine looked sympathetic. "None of us are being very helpful, are we? Summer Island is turning out to be a bit of a bust. Do you think you'll head back to New York early?"

"Is that a hint?" Despite her lack of cooperation, he couldn't help liking Justine. She was being honest. And not unfriendly. He got the feeling that normally she was a very forthright person.

Justine smiled. "I'm sure I'm not the first one to tell you we'd rather you didn't write this book."

"No. You're not the first. But even if every resident of Summer Island signed a petition, it wouldn't be enough to stop me."

"Yes. The word on the street is that you're the tenacious sort." She scooped some papers into her briefcase, then fastened the clasp. "Well, I'm finished here. Sorry I couldn't be of more help. Really, I am."

He believed her. "That's okay. I understand that you'd want to be loyal to your friend."

A funny look crossed over Justine's face. "I assume you're talking about Jennifer. She's the one who cares about this the most. For the record, Simone and I were never friends. I don't have the same capacity for forgiveness that Jennifer does."

BY SUNSET NICK STILL HADN'T returned to the B and B. Jennifer tried not to speculate on where he might be, as she climbed into the old pickup and headed for the beach.

Clouds on the western horizon blocked the sunset tonight and swaying treetops warned Jennifer the wind was picking up. She turned on the radio, hoping for a weather report. Five minutes later her suspicions were confirmed when the announcer predicted scattered thundershowers among the Gulf Islands. Hopefully the Watertons, out on their kayaking expedition, would set up camp before the rain hit.

Harrison's and Gabe's vehicles were the only cars parked at Pebble Beach when Jennifer arrived. She pulled up next to Harrison's dark green SUV, then cut her engine. Down by the beach the flickering flames of a bonfire rose up into the darkening sky. Next to the fire were three masculine silhouettes.

How long had the guys been down there without a mediator? She grabbed her jacket, then hurried to join them.

Harrison and Gabe had barely spoken to each other since Simone's funeral three years ago. It was strange to see them now, sitting within a few feet of one another. Harrison was tall and large-boned, a big man with broad shoulders and strong, almost coarse features. Though he was handsome in a rugged way, in a contest based on appearances alone, he would always be outshone by Gabe or Aidan.

While Gabe was the island golden boy, Aidan was as dark as Gabe was fair. His hair was almost black, his eyes a deep, mysterious brown.

"Sorry I'm late," she said. They looked relieved to see her and she guessed the atmosphere had been as tense among them as she'd feared.

Which was sad. They'd been so close once. They were still among her favorite people in the world. Individually, she knew she could count on any one of them if she needed help. But as a group they no longer shared the same connection.

"You're not late," Harrison assured her. "We're early." He gestured at the clouds. "I'm thinking we're in for some rain tonight."

"That's what the weather report just said." She slipped on her jacket against the cool breeze, then sat on the log next to Harrison, purposefully creating a buffer zone between him and Gabe.

Aidan tossed another log onto the growing fire. "You okay, Jenn?" There was a hint of curiosity in his eyes as he smiled at her and she quickly turned away. Of the three guys, Aidan had always been the one to read her best, and she didn't want him to see the inner turmoil she'd been battling.

She wanted Nick gone, yet she'd spent all day anxious for the sight of him. What was the matter with her?

"Well, here we all are," Gabe said, his tone as dry as the wine in the glass he'd handed her. Everyone else already had some, she noticed. "The forget-me-not friends."

All but Simone. And Emerson.

Jennifer looked up to the sky. Once, when they were kids, Simone had made a fanciful comment about turning into a star when she was dead. There was something comforting about the notion.

But there were no stars visible tonight. Dark clouds were shifting and jostling for position in the approaching storm. Jennifer shivered, although she wasn't cold. "I thought Nessa was coming. And Rae and Justine."

"They decided the original four of us should handle this," Harrison explained. "Whatever we decide, they'll go along with."

"Well, I can see an easy solution to the

whole situation," Gabe said. "All Jennifer needs to do is kick him out of the bed-and-breakfast. I'll make sure no one else on the island has room for him."

Jennifer sensed all three men looking at her, waiting for her reaction.

"I can't believe you booked him into Lavender Farm in the first place," Gabe added.

"She didn't know what he was up to when he registered." Aidan was quick to come to her defense.

"But now she does."

"This isn't Jennifer's fault," Harrison said. "It isn't anyone's fault."

"I wasn't implying—"

"It's okay," Jennifer said quickly. "I was mad, too, when I found out what Nick was really doing on the island. But Nick's put a lot of research into this project. Nothing's going to make him give it up."

"If he didn't have a place to stay—"

"I can't kick him out. I already tried. My father and Annie like him. And they don't understand why I'm so opposed to this book."

"Speaking of the book," Harrison said. "I wonder if at least a show of cooperation might get us further ahead. Since we're agreed we can't stop Nick from writing it, we could at least control some of his information."

"I don't agree." Gabe struck a rebellious pose. "And I'm really surprised that you think that way. Have you thought about your sister? Nessa isn't going to appreciate being reminded of that period of our lives."

"You're underestimating my sister. She's over it, Gabe. She's moved on with her life like I have. And like you should, too."

"Harrison's right," Aidan said. "It's about time that we—"

Gabe made a sneering noise. "Big surprise, Aidan's agreeing with Harrison. Who would have guessed?"

"This isn't about taking sides." Jennifer couldn't believe them. Couldn't they talk for fifteen minutes without getting confrontational? Justine, Nessa and Rae had been wrong not to come. Their presence would have helped keep the peace. Or at least a semblance of peace. "Please, don't let's get into a fight over this."

To her surprise, Gabe apologized. "Jennifer's right. Let's keep this civil. But I'm still not convinced cooperation is the right approach."

"Neither am I," Jennifer agreed. "We have nothing to gain by helping Nick. He'll find enough information from other sources to write his book. I'd hate to think that the public might consider this biography endorsed by Simone's closest friends."

"You seem pretty set on that."

"I am. I don't like this, Harrison. I really don't."

"Well, you've spent the most time with this Nick Lancaster. That should count for something. Is there anything else you think we should watch out for? Justine said he cornered her at her office this morning. He was asking about the forget-me-not song."

"Of course," Aidan sighed. "Well, none of us can help him with that, can we?"

Jennifer said nothing. They'd talked about this subject before. Privately Simone had told each of Gabe, Harrison and Aidan—as well as Emerson—that her song had been written with him in mind. Nick would never discover the truth.

"I bet he'll be looking for answers about Simone's mother," Gabe said.

"Didn't you try to track her down, Harrison?" Aidan asked.

"I offered to hire a private investigator, many times, but Simone wouldn't let me. She was afraid to find out the truth, in case it was something she couldn't handle. That was the one thing that always kept her going…writing songs, making records, performing. In the back of her mind she always dreamed that one day her mother was going to hear one of her songs and come find her."

"We don't even know if Simone's mother is dead or alive," Jennifer said.

"Not for sure," Harrison said. "But the sort of woman who would run out on a young daughter is probably the same type who would show up on the scene when that daughter struck it rich. So I think it's pretty certain that Andrea DeRosier is dead."

All of them nodded and at that moment lightning snaked from one cloud to the next. A few seconds later, thunder grumbled.

The storm was coming.

"I've got to get going," Gabe said. "I'm supposed to meet someone."

Jennifer looked into the faces of her three old friends. *What a sad sight.* No one smiled. Gabe and Harrison still avoided looking at one another. She threw the rest of her wine into the sand. "So we're agreed? No one's going to help with this book?"

One by one, each of the guys gave her their word.

"We better get out of here before the rain starts." Harrison dumped the remainder of his wine on the fire, then kicked sand into the flames. Soon the fire was doused.

Everyone was silent as they made their way back to their vehicles. Gabe was the first out of the parking lot, driving as if he was in a real hurry. Aidan opened the door of the pickup for Jenn.

"You'll keep an eye on that fellow, Jenn?" he said. "Let us know if we need to revise the plan?"

She nodded.

"Great. Drive careful." Aidan shut the door, then headed to Harrison's SUV.

As JENNIFER NOSED THE truck onto the main road, the storm crashed onto the island. Rain fell in a steady downpour. Thunder followed lightning in the wink of an eye. Harrison waved her over, opening his side window to yell at her.

"Come to the house! It's raining too hard for you to drive all the way home."

The Kincaid summerhouse was just half a mile from the beach, much closer than the B and B.

"Okay!" she hollered, hoping he'd hear her above the roaring of the storm. She rolled up her window quickly, already drenched.

She followed behind Harrison's SUV, pausing when it came time to park in the driveway. On the opposite side of the street she could make out the outline of another vehicle. Its boxy shape looked familiar. As she drove past she saw Nick Lancaster's New York plates.

She pulled a U-turn then parked behind the Rover. Zipping up her coat and slipping the hood over her head, she stepped outside. The rain was coming so hard, she could barely see. She waved at Harrison and Aidan on the other side of the road.

"I'm going to Molly's."

They couldn't hear her, so she pointed toward the small cottage. They nodded, then hurried inside to their waiting wives and children.

Jennifer walked around to the driver's side door of Nick's vehicle. The windows were fogged over, making it difficult to see inside, so she tried the door. It was unlocked.

Nick was there. Sitting in the driver's seat. Asleep.

He jumped when he felt the rain hit the side of his face. His eyes shot open wide when he saw Jennifer.

"What the hell—"

Jennifer scooted around the vehicle to the passenger side. She slipped inside, shutting the door quickly. Water ran in streams off her waterproof jacket. She pulled down the hood and shook yet more water onto the Rover's seat.

"What are you doing here, Nick?"

Nick still looked stunned as he rubbed a hand over his face. "Right back at you, Jenn. Where the hell did you come from?"

"I was—" She felt a bite of conscience, and that made her angry. She had nothing to feel guilty about. "I was meeting some friends on the beach when the storm blew up and we ran for cover."

"Friends...?"

She could see the questions forming in his mind. But she had questions of her own. Why was he parked here outside of Molly's house? "You're spying on her, aren't you?"

The frustrating man just stared back at her, impassive.

"I don't get it." She peered out the fogged windshield toward the yoga studio. All the lights were out, except for the front porch. Molly couldn't be home. Which meant Nick was waiting for her.

Again, she could only wonder why. "Molly didn't even know Simone..."

She looked at Nick again, expectantly.

"Go home, Jennifer." He sounded tired. "You don't want to get in the middle of this."

The middle of *what?* "I'm not leaving until you give me an answer. Molly is a good friend. And you're *stalking* her. Maybe I should call the police."

"Oh, brilliant." Nick rolled his eyes. "I'm not doing anything wrong. Just waiting for her to come home. Where do you think she could be at this hour anyway?"

"I don't know. It's Saturday night. Maybe she has a date."

"You're probably right," Nick said. "If she's out for dinner or something she won't be back for hours. No sense me sitting here in the rain for that long. I'll have to try and talk to her another time."

"What are you so anxious to talk to her about?"

"Jennifer…"

"I'm serious. I'm not leaving until you give me some answers." It wasn't fair that he grilled her with questions all the time, but never reciprocated when the tables were turned.

"I don't have answers to give you. Not yet, anyway." He stared at Molly's house, his mouth set. "She's been in the picture since I began this project and I still have no clue why."

"What do you mean? Nick, have you met Molly before?"

CHAPTER TWELVE

NICK SIGHED AS IF HE WAS about to start a long story. "I started working on this book three years ago. Not full time, I was putting the finishing touches on my last book. But I began the research, starting at the end, rather than the beginning."

"With Simone's death," Jennifer prompted.

"That's right. First the suicide verdict, then a year later, the surprising murder revelation. It was more the stuff of pulp fiction novels than thoughtful biographies, but I was intrigued by the contradictions in her personality. And I was sure that there had to be more to the story than what met the eye."

He'd been right. "But how does this tie into Molly?"

"I'm getting there. In my preliminary research stage I talked to Simone's agent, to a few of the musicians who had worked with her, to journalists who had covered her career."

Oh, God. He'd been very thorough if that was what he considered *preliminary* research.

"Everywhere I went, I heard the same thing. *Funny you should ask. We just had a woman come round with the same questions.*"

"Molly?"

"Yes."

"And this was in New York City? Not Toronto?"

"That's right. I couldn't figure out what she was after. I tried to talk to her, but the one time I actually managed to introduce myself, she slipped away on me."

Jennifer sank back against the hard seat of the Rover. This couldn't be right. Nick had Molly mixed up with someone else.

But little bits and pieces were falling into place. Like Molly's insatiable curiosity about Simone. And her reluctance to talk about her past. Suddenly it seemed entirely plausible that Molly was hiding something. And she'd done so for much longer than the single day that Nick had concealed his true purpose.

Jennifer felt sick to her stomach. "Do you think she's writing a book, too?"

"I don't know. If so, it would be her first. She doesn't have any publishing history. I've checked."

Jennifer peered through the rain at Molly's house.

"She bought this place because of the location. Because it was across from Simone's summer home, didn't she?" This thing just got bigger and bigger the more she thought about it. "Molly moved to this island, to this house, on purpose."

"I think so."

"But why?" she asked again.

"Molly's *your* friend. Why don't *you* ask her?"

"She's been avoiding me lately." Suddenly it all made sense to Jennifer.

"Ever since that day you picked me up outside her yoga studio. She must have seen you. Recognized you."

"Probably."

"Is that why she's put her house up for sale? Because you came to the island?" The guy in Ontario was a ruse. And the dinners out with Gabe? Who knew what those were about. Probably not just business as Molly had claimed.

"The timing seems too suspicious for anything else. But I don't understand why she sees me as such a threat."

They both fell silent then. Jennifer struggled to come to terms with the fact that the woman she'd considered a friend had moved here under false pretenses. What was her secret? And why *was* she so desperate to avoid Nick?

Had Molly sought her out as a friend because of her ties to Simone? Had she been pumping Jennifer for information these past few years without Jennifer even guessing what she was about?

Her head started to ache. It was too much.

"Poor Jennifer," Nick said softly. "You've always counted so much on your friends. You don't deserve any of this."

An odd stillness settled over them. The rain had stopped.

Nick started the motor and turned on the defrost. Quickly the condensation on the windows cleared.

"I'd better get home."

"I'll follow," Nick said as she stepped out to the mushy earth. She kept hold of the passenger door for a moment. She felt a little lightheaded, as if she'd been lying down in a dark room and had just stepped into the sun.

"You've had a shock," Nick said. "Maybe you should ride home with me and we can come back for your truck tomorrow."

"I'm fine," she insisted. She jumped over puddles on her way to her pickup. The air was cool and fresh now and she pulled off her soaked jacket and stowed it on the passenger seat. As she drove off, she kept an eye on the rearview mirror.

True to his word, Nick was following in her tracks.

Behind him, Molly's house remained silent and dark.

THOUGH HE'D ARRIVED AT THE restaurant fifteen minutes late, Molly had had a wonderful time at dinner with Gabe. After, he took her to his house for an espresso made with a beautiful Italian machine built right into the cherry cabinetry of his kitchen. He had the most gorgeous house on the island, all huge windows and cedar, nestled into the cliff on which it had been built.

Molly stood in front of the windows in the living room. "The view must be spectacular in the daytime."

Gabe came up from behind her and passed her the delicate cup of espresso. She turned to face him. Her heart twisted at the sight of him, his gorgeous blue eyes focused so intensely on her.

Why couldn't this thing have sparked between them earlier...like a year earlier?

It was so unfair that he'd finally noticed her just when she realized she had to move on.

"I had fun tonight," she said. As she had the previous night, too. If Gabe was trying to sweep her off her feet, he was definitely succeeding.

"Likewise. You look very alluring tonight, Molly."

Alluring. Trust a newspaperman to come up with a word like that. But she liked it. *Alluring.* Yes, she liked it a lot. She took a sip of coffee. "This was supposed to be a business dinner, wasn't it?"

Gabe laughed softly. "Is that what you feel like discussing right now? Business?"

He slipped his arms around her waist. Suddenly the little cup and saucer in her hand felt like a huge impediment. Gabe seemed to read her mind. He took it from her hands and set it on the windowsill.

And then he kissed her.

And my, oh my, did Gabe Brooke know how to kiss a woman.

"Gabe," she breathed.

"I love your hair." He combed his fingers into it, and she felt a slight tugging on her scalp.

"Watch out. You're trapped now. You'll never get your fingers out of there."

"Sounds fine by me." He kissed her again, until she couldn't keep anything straight. Certainly not any of her thoughts.

"We'd better sit down," Gabe said. "You should finish your coffee before it gets cold."

Molly didn't care about her coffee. But the sitting down sounded fine. She sank into a leather sofa that faced the river-rock fireplace. Gabe handed her the cup again, then went back into the kitchen to get his own.

He was putting on the brakes, she realized. But why? Hadn't he enjoyed kissing her? The idea filled her with insecurity.

But when he returned, he immediately settled those fears.

"I think we should do this again," he said. "Are you free next weekend?"

"I'm not sure I can wait that long."

He laughed. "God, I love your honesty."

Her conscience gave her a hard poke. "I'm not always so honest, Gabe. Are you?"

"I try to be." He gave her a speculative look. "What are you not so honest about?"

"Oh, things. My family. I don't like to talk about them very much." She cringed inwardly at the airbrushed answer, but Gabe seemed to accept it.

"Who *does* like talking about their family? Not me."

"Why not? Don't you get along?"

"Since Dad and Mom retired to Arizona, I hardly see them." Gabe shrugged. "It's probably for the best. Dad and I always butt heads when we spend too much time together."

"Gabe, can I ask you something kind of personal?"

"You asked me something personal the first time you met me, as I recall. Go ahead."

He must be talking about the night on the beach when she'd tried to figure out which of the forget-me-not friends Simone had written her song for. It was still a question that puzzled her. Quite likely the real truth would never be known.

But something else was bothering Molly more right now. "Did you really love Simone? Everyone says you did. Are they right?"

For a second she was afraid she'd blown everything. Hurt flashed in Gabe's eyes, followed by a different emotion she couldn't identify.

"I don't like to talk about Simone."

"I'm sorry."

"But maybe it's good to get this out in the open. My friends were just telling me it's time I moved on, and I think I'm more than ready to do that."

"Good," she encouraged.

"The sad truth is my feelings for Simone destroyed my first marriage. But whether I loved Simone or not, I still couldn't tell you. One thing's for sure, I was obsessed with her. And my pride was involved, too. I was determined to be the man she picked. Determined that eventually she would leave Harrison for me. Whether that qualifies as love, I don't know. I'll leave that for you to judge."

Molly wasn't sure she could. But what counted were his feelings now, not those from the past. "Do you still miss her?"

He seemed surprised by the question. He thought for a moment, then angled his head. "You know, I don't think that I do. I haven't thought of her, except in a superficial sense, in ages."

"I see." Guilt weighted down her response. Gabe was being so honest and open, but she couldn't return the favor. The secret she was living with simply wasn't hers to tell.

He took her hands and held them tightly. "Now you answer a question for me. Do you really want to leave Summer Island? I had two queries about your cottage today. I shouldn't admit this, but I almost didn't return the calls. I don't want you to move, Molly."

Her heart danced. "Summer Island is suddenly looking a lot more attractive than it did last week," she admitted.

If only Nick Lancaster would give up and go back where he belonged. But as she'd told Jennifer, that wasn't very likely to happen.

THE NEXT MORNING JENNIFER was anxious to go to her yoga class and talk to Molly. But when her aunt asked for her company on a trip to Cedarbrae to see the doctor and pick up a refill of her arthritis medication, she couldn't say no. During breakfast she'd noticed how slowly Annie had eaten…as if it pained her just to pick up her fork.

They were an hour and a half in Cedarbrae and on the way home, Annie insisted on stopping at the Kincaid house to visit Rae and Aidan and their baby, Layton. Annie and Rae had bonded last summer when Rae had come to the island to rest before the birth. At that time she and Aidan had barely been speaking to each other, let alone prepared to become parents to a new baby boy.

A lot could change in a year or two, Jennifer thought, as she sat on the Kincaids' deck with her friends and her aunt, holding Erica on her lap. Three years ago, when Simone had been found asphyxiated on the front seat of her Mercedes in the garage that used to sit on this property, Jennifer had felt as if the world had ended.

Yet life had gone on. The people who loved Simone most had recovered. Even her husband had found happiness and fulfillment again.

"More iced tea, Jenn?" Justine filled her glass then passed the plate of homemade cookies. Jennifer accepted one and bit into it with pleasure. She felt slightly decadent being waited upon like this. But it made a nice change.

She watched as Annie held Layton's hand and led the newly mobile baby wherever he wanted to go. Annie was completely besotted with the little boy, who could do no wrong in her eyes. Not even when he pulled the blossoms off one of Justine's potted plants.

Justine just winced and looked away.

Jennifer jiggled her knee and Erica giggled. Harrison and Justine's baby had a few dried sores on her face, but other than that, she was acting like her normal self. "Erica seems fully recovered."

"She better be," Justine said. "I'll feel really guilty if Layton gets sick."

"He's been vaccinated, so no worries." Rae had her long dark hair up in a bun. With her dramatic eyes and long, lithe body, she looked more like a ballet dancer than a corporate mogul. Yet she and Aidan were in charge of Mergers and Acquisitions at Kincaid Communications.

"So, Jennifer. Did you and the guys figure out how to deal with this biographer last night?" Justine asked.

She met Harrison's gaze, then Aidan's. They both gave a slight nod. "We did."

"I hope a cement block, some rope and a long walk down a short pier are part of the plan," Rae said.

"Rae!" Aidan shook his head at his wife. "We've got children present."

Jennifer couldn't help but laugh. Rae spoke her mind, just like Molly.... Jennifer turned to Justine. "What do you know about Molly before she lived on the island?"

Justine wiped a trail of dribble from Erica's mouth. "Well, she moved here from Toronto. Said she wanted to make a fresh start after the death of her mother."

"Has her interest in Simone ever seemed...excessive to you?"

Everyone, even the guys who'd gone back to their discussion of share prices, turned quiet at Jennifer's question.

"Actually, yes," Justine said. "I remember she was very keen to get a look inside this house when she first moved into the neighborhood. Also, I thought it was strange that even when I found a bigger property at a better price, she insisted on buying the Wythe cottage."

"Remember the commotion she caused on the beach two years ago?" Aidan added. "She was so determined to find out which of us Simone had in mind when she wrote that song."

"Why are you asking, Jenn?" Justine said thoughtfully. "Is there something about Molly we don't know?"

Jennifer hesitated, then decided against telling them what Nick had said last night. She'd give Molly a chance to explain things before she spoke out against her.

IT WAS ALMOST TEATIME when Jennifer and her aunt returned to the B and B. Claiming fatigue, Annie went to her cottage for her nap. Jennifer slipped in the back door and filled the kettle with water. As she turned off the tap, her father entered the room.

"You were gone a long time." He squeezed her shoulder affectionately, then started pulling cups and saucers from the cupboard. "Did your aunt get her medicine?"

"Yes. We stopped in at the Kincaids' house for a while." She plugged in the kettle, then picked a lemon from the fruit bowl to slice for the tea. "What have you been up to?"

There was a comfort and a warmth to preparing the afternoon tea with her father. It was a routine they'd shared countless times.

"You know that leak in the far bedroom?"

"Yes." One of the guests had complained this morning. Apparently last night's storm had been too much for the old roof.

Jennifer watched her father shuffle to the sideboard with the dishes. He'd done his best not to let his disability slow him down. But there were some limitations he had to learn to accept—especially now that he was older.

"You didn't try to fix that on your own, did you?"

"Nick helped."

She froze, her knife poised over the lemon. "Did he go up in the attic?"

"Sure. Only way to fix the leak, isn't it? You wouldn't believe what we found up there."

Oh, Jennifer could believe all right. Years ago when they'd added the rooms over the garage, she'd moved the plastic storage tubs to the attic.

"Dad, you didn't—"

"Nick's in the living room right now looking through your old photo albums."

She dropped the knife.

"I didn't think you'd mind. They're just pictures, Jennifer."

JENNIFER PAUSED IN THE doorway watching as Nick flipped through the album she'd made in her last year of high school, amalgamating all the pictures and mementoes she'd collected during her teen years. Disbelief morphed into outrage as she wondered if Nick had offered to help her father, perhaps hoping he'd find something useful for his book.

He'd obviously been well rewarded for his efforts.

"What the hell do you think you're doing?"

Nick lifted his head, startled by her

voice. Before he could say anything, her father came up behind her.

"You've got some excellent shots of Simone," he said. "Maybe Nick can use some of them in his book."

"Oh, I'll just bet Nick would love to use them." She crossed the room in several strides and snatched the album from Nick's hands. She looked back at her father. "Dad, these are private."

"What do you mean? There's nothing wrong with them. Just kids goofing off and having fun." Her father brushed a hand over his stiff gray hair. "I told Nick he'd need to get your permission if he wanted to use any of them."

"Oh, Dad." He just didn't get it, but she couldn't blame him. He didn't know what was at stake. Nick was the one who should have known better. But he'd already demonstrated that he had no scruples. At least not where his precious book was at stake.

He still hadn't said a word. Well, what could he possibly say? Nothing could defend what he had done.

But the way he was looking at her made her heart sink.

He'd seen it. She had no doubt about it.

Clutching the album to her chest, she said, "I'm going to my room."

"But the tea—"

"Sorry, Dad. This one you'll have to handle on your own."

CHAPTER THIRTEEN

JENNIFER FLOPPED ONTO HER bed, still holding the album close to her chest. She was so angry at Nick, she wanted to scream. He'd had no right to look at these pictures. No right at all.

Silently she fumed on her bed until she judged that tea was over. Then she went searching for her father. She found him in the living room, working on a crossword.

"Dad, we need to talk."

He peered at her from over his glasses.

"I know you like Nick, Dad. But Simone was *my* friend and those pictures are from *my* life."

He put up a hand to stop her. "You're right, Jennifer. I'm sorry I showed him your albums. I shouldn't have done that."

"No. You shouldn't have. Just be careful what you give him in the future, okay? And tell Annie to be careful as well."

"I will. But Jennifer, he's a good man. I don't think he'll print anything you don't want him to."

Jennifer said nothing to that, though she was quite sure her father was absolutely wrong.

NICK HAD DECLINED PHIL'S offer for tea and gone up to his room to work. He liked this room, found it a good, quiet place to write. And the pastoral view provided inspiration during lulls in his thinking process. But today he didn't do anything, just sat in his chair and stared out at the view. He still couldn't get his mind around what he'd found in Jennifer's album.

Was it really possible?

Had Jennifer—not Simone—written the lyrics to the forget-me-not song?

The evidence was in her album, in a note she'd written to her friend, Simone. The entire chorus was there, word for word just like in the song. *You see a comet cross the sky, you make a wish, it passes by; but will you remember me at the brilliant end?*

Forget me not, my one true friend.

It was Simone's most famous song. The one that had launched her career. But it had been signed by Jennifer.

Below the note was a return message from Simone.

Of course I'll never forget you, Jenn. But nice poem. I'd like to set it to music.

Do you really think it's good enough?

Yeah, I do. It's really good.

At the time Jennifer couldn't have had any idea what she'd just written—the lyrics to a song that would earn millions, along with a Grammy Award and much fame.

And what had Jennifer received in return? Nick was willing to bet, not very much.

A movement in the gardens below caught his eye. Edging closer to the window, he noticed Jennifer walking purposefully through the back gardens. It looked like she was heading toward the old barn.

He raced down the stairs, then dashed outside, but he wasn't fast enough to catch her. Going on his hunch, he headed for the barn. The building hadn't been used for livestock in years, he guessed, judging by the gaps between the old boards, which had weathered to a silvery gray. The door was missing, too, and he halted at the threshold, waiting before going any farther.

Jennifer was wrapping bunches of lavender with twine, then stringing them to the rafters, presumably so they would dry. She'd tied her hair back in a ponytail that swayed from one tanned shoulder to the other as she worked.

The large open space of the barn was filled with the sweet, old-fashioned scent of lavender, and Nick knew he'd never smell the perfume again without thinking of this woman.

He took a step inside and his footstep sounded loud on the old concrete. Jennifer's ponytail whipped to the opposite shoulder as she turned in his direction.

For a moment she just stared, her hostility obvious. He hated that he had been the one to make her so miserable.

Maybe he should have left that album alone. But it would have taken a bigger man than he was to say no when Phil had asked if he wanted to take a look through it.

"Are you okay?"

She shook her head at him, as if she couldn't believe he'd even asked.

"I'm sorry," he said, belatedly.

Her eyes narrowed. "You have no limits, do you?"

"That's a little harsh."

"Using an old man like that…"

"Hey, I saw him pull out a ladder and I

offered to help. Did you really want your dad going up in that attic alone?"

He saw her struggle with that.

"Well, thanks," she said grudgingly, "But you didn't have to look at that album."

"I didn't know what was up there. Your father saw the storage tubs and he *offered*. Do you really think anyone in my position would turn him down?"

"Those albums belong to me. Not my father."

"He didn't make that distinction when he asked if I wanted to take a look."

"My father was being friendly. Something you were only too quick to take advantage of. Just as you've been using me. Since the first minute you got here."

She wrapped her arms around her waist, and she looked so lovely, so pretty and vulnerable and…hurt, that Nick felt a physical ache in his chest.

Something was going wrong here. Jennifer was supposed to be a source of information for his book. Nothing more. So why did he feel so shitty right now? Why did the book—the all-important book—suddenly feel just a little less significant than it had a day or two ago?

And why did it matter so much what this woman thought of him?

"Jenn, it wasn't like that. Your father is an intelligent man with full possession of his faculties. I helped him with something and he reciprocated by letting me look at an old album he thought I'd find interesting. He had no idea what I'd find in there."

Jennifer blanched and he knew he'd just confirmed that he'd seen the note.

He softened his voice. "Did you ever get credited for those lyrics or receive any royalties for that song?"

"I don't care about the money. Or getting credit. Simone wrote the music and she sang the song. She's the one who made it into a big hit. Not me."

"Yes. But that's not the point. You *did* write the lyrics?"

"Yes, but Simone was always so generous with me. She paid for all my trips. And bought me the most extravagant presents. You've seen the Emily Carr original, but I have other things, too."

"Jenn. The money isn't the most important thing, but sure, let's start with that. A dozen Emily Carr originals wouldn't scratch the surface of what your share of profits would have been if you'd been named cowriter of that song."

She turned away. "Are you saying Simone cheated me?"

"How do you see it, Jenn?"

"If she hadn't decided to turn my little poem into a song, nothing would have happened with it. It was Simone's talent, Simone's drive that made that song a hit."

"And you didn't ever want to claim any credit—not even a tiny little bit—for your contribution?"

"You don't understand—"

"You're right. I don't. For years people have been trying to figure out who Simone wanted to remember her...but those weren't even her words. The song is about you. About your wanting to hang on to a friend as she's about to be catapulted into a world of success and fame beyond your imagination. Isn't that right?"

Without looking at him she nodded.

The big puzzle he'd come here to solve had turned out to be a complete misdirection. In a way it was disappointing. He'd really hoped that the song would provide an important insight into Simone's character. But in a way it did. It proved that Simone's ambition had been so ruthless, she'd been willing to pursue her fame at the expense of one of her closest friends.

"You deserved better, Jenn."

She swallowed. Started to back up. But he reached her before she had a chance to put much space between them. He took her hands and raised them to his face. They were dirty with lavender dust, but still soft and pretty and fragile.

Like Jennifer.

"Let go of me."

He did as she asked, but didn't step out of her personal space. "What will you do if I print the truth in my book? Will you try to deny it?"

She looked like she wanted to say yes, but couldn't. Jennifer's inherent honesty was working against her now. And Nick knew that he had won.

So why did he still feel so terrible?

OVER THE NEXT COUPLE WEEKS, Nick spent a lot of time on the phone and at the library doing research. Jennifer knew this, because when her errands took her into Cedarbrae she would see his vehicle parked in the lot next to the island library. A couple of times she almost went inside on the pretense of borrowing a few books, but in the end, she resisted.

She went to yoga class as usual, but Molly managed to busy herself in conversations with others at the end of each workout. Clearly she did not want to discuss her decision to move or her connection with Nick.

Jennifer tried not to feel hurt, but it was difficult—especially when she noticed

Gabe and Molly eating together at Derby's one day. Gabe smiled and waved at her, but Molly was decidedly cool.

The message Molly was sending was obvious. She didn't want to talk to her. And maybe it was just as well. Jennifer was still trying to recover from Nick's discovery of her own secret. No one in the world knew that she had written that verse. No one but Nick. And she wondered if others would see the situation the way he did.

Had Simone cheated her?

But she'd asked for permission to use Jennifer's words, and Jennifer had given it to her. She'd given it wholeheartedly, without any lingering resentment or feelings of entitlement.

Still, the question Nick had asked was one she couldn't get out of her mind. *You didn't ever want to claim any credit—not even a tiny little bit—for your contribution?* She realized that the one thing that had bothered her most was the way Simone had told each of the guys that she'd written the song for them. More than any royalties, or public acclaim, that more personal betrayal was what burned the most.

And Nick knew it.

She'd been staying out of his way since their talk in the barn. He thought she was still angry about the album, and she was. But she was avoiding him for more reasons than just that.

The real problem here was the way she felt about him. When he'd taken her hands, she'd been flooded with a desire that she couldn't understand. Why was she drawn to a man who had no scruples, who was out to expose her, who kept making her think about things that belonged in her past?

It seemed like the more she steered clear of him, the more she thought of him. Especially at night. She'd lie in bed and listen to the creaking of the old house and imagine him just up the stairs and down the hall from her.

Time was passing so quickly now. In

less than ten days, he'd be back in New York City. Was she crazy to be wasting precious opportunities to spend time with him? She could see in his eyes that he felt this attraction, too. If she'd been a different kind of woman, she had no doubt that they could be in the midst of an exciting affair right now. And though their relationship would be brief, at least she'd have an adventure to think about in the years to come.

Unfortunately she wasn't a different kind of woman. She couldn't blithely step into a sexual relationship with a man she didn't trust. She might as well accept that she was fated to be quiet, dependable Jennifer March for the rest of her life.

On the third Friday of September, just after she'd cleared the answering machine of messages from people seeking reservations, there was a knock at the front door.

She wasn't supposed to be getting any new guests today. And Nick had just left— she presumed to go to the library again. Jennifer opened the door, half expecting to find one of her neighbors collecting money for charity.

But it was the FedEx delivery man. And he had an envelope for Nick.

Jennifer signed for it, then took the package up to his room. She stood in the doorway for a long time, turning the envelope around and around in her hands, wondering what might be in there. It was obviously a document of some sort.

Something to do with the book?

She'd bet money on it.

She wanted so badly to open the envelope. Didn't she have the right? After all, he'd snooped through her private collage of postcards and her photo albums.

But this wasn't the same, and reluctantly, she set the unopened envelope on his desk and left his room, closing the door firmly behind her.

That night when Nick came home for tea, she tried to keep her voice casual when she told him about it. "By the way, there was a FedEx delivery for you today. The envelope is on your desk."

Nick's eyes lit up. Clearly he'd been waiting for something. He got up, leaving his food untouched on the table.

She watched him go, and her curiosity burned.

"Foolish man putting work before fresh strawberries and English scones." Her father dumped a spoonful of thick cream onto his own plate, before passing the jar to Jennifer.

Jennifer took a little, then passed it on to Annie. *Foolish.* Yes, her father was right. Only the adjective applied to her more than it did to Nick.

NICK HAD BEEN ANTICIPATING a report from the investigator he'd hired and as soon as he saw the return address on the package, he knew this was it. He had no idea what the report contained—they'd been playing telephone tag for several days—but he was hopeful.

Two weeks ago he'd been so dis-couraged about this project. Now, finally, things were turning around. He ripped the package open and dumped the contents out on the desk. Within a few minutes, he had his answer, and he was stunned.

Strangely, his first thought wasn't for the impact this would have on his book. It was for Jennifer.

She's going to be so hurt...

But he couldn't worry about that. It wasn't his fault that Molly had lied to her friends. He had a book to write and he had to keep his focus where it belonged.

Picking up the phone, he dialed Molly's number, which he'd long ago memorized, since he called it so often leaving messages that were never returned. He wasn't surprised when she didn't answer, but this time he left a different message than his usual.

"Hey, Molly. This is Nick Lancaster. Just wanted to let you know that I know who you really are. I'll give you a day to tell your friends the truth. But that's all. If you want to reach me, you know the number."

NICK LEFT FOR CEDARBRAE early the next morning. Right after he drove off, Justine showed up at the bed-and-breakfast, dressed in old jeans, prepared to spend a day in the gardens.

"I didn't think you were serious," Jennifer said.

"Sure I was. I owe you big time. Harrison's with the baby and Autumn is playing with Tyler at Nessa's. So give me a job, any job."

Jennifer grabbed a pair of gardening gloves and a hoe from the shed and led Justine to a particularly weedy patch of the garden.

"So where's Nick Lancaster this morning?" Justine asked, after Jennifer had showed her what to do.

"He left for town right after breakfast."

"Did he tell you he came by to have a drink at our house a couple days ago?"

"Really? Did he and Harrison come to blows?"

Justine laughed. "Actually it was all very civil. Harrison even let him have a box of Simone's papers."

"Interesting." Slowly, he was getting to

know all of them. Every one of the forget-me-not gang. And Jennifer was willing to bet he was learning a lot more from each of them than they guessed he was.

Jennifer left Justine in the garden, and as she went about her morning work she tried not to dwell on her feelings of resentment—or her growing curiosity about that FedEx envelope.

Once the kitchen was clean, Jennifer decided to replenish the towels in the bathroom suite. She gave two bath sheets a final spritz of lavender water, then carried them up the stairs.

At Nick's closed door, she felt a twinge of guilt, which she firmly pushed aside. She was merely doing her job. She was *not* snooping.

She went through the neat bedroom to the bathroom and replaced the damp towels with the clean ones. As she folded them just so, she noticed the razor on the edge of the sink, the brush with several of Nick's dark hairs caught within the bristles.

Oh my Lord, I'm turning into a stalker.

She was backing out of the room, when her glance caught the wastepaper basket by Nick's desk.

It was stuffed to overflowing.

A cleaning woman came in every other day. Part of her job was to empty all trash containers. Jennifer never did this. No way could she justify, to herself or anyone else, inspecting a guest's garbage.

But even as Jennifer thought these noble thoughts, she was inching her way toward the alcove where the desk was positioned to make best use of the light.

Finally she was close enough to peer inside.

No FedEx envelope.

So…where was it?

Nick's desk, like the room, was scrupulously tidy. His laptop was missing, but then he usually took it with him when he went out for the day. The box of files was closed. She didn't dare look inside that.

She had to leave while she still had any scruples left at all. She scanned the room one last time.

Whoa. It was so obvious, she couldn't believe she'd missed it when she'd first entered the room. On the cushioned window seat on the other side of the bed, out in plain view for anyone to see, was the FedEx envelope. Beside it lay a sheaf of papers.

Jennifer moved in closer. Without touching anything, she read the cover page. It was a letter from an investigative firm in Toronto, addressed to Mr. Nicolaus Lancaster.

We are pleased to report that we have completed the comprehensive background check on Molly Eleanor Springfield, as per your request.

Jennifer scanned through the rest of the cover letter. Some details about payment and expenses followed, ending with a promise to follow up with a phone call.

She fingered the corner of the page. Did she dare flip the letter over and read the actual report?

"I guess we're even now."

She gasped at the sound of Nick's voice. He was in the doorway, briefcase in hand.

She stared at him mutely. How could he be back so soon? She'd seen him leave for the day. He didn't usually return before teatime.

He set the briefcase on the floor by his desk. "I can't believe you would actually search my room."

She could have defended herself. After all, she hadn't touched anything. But then she remembered that he had snooped through her things, too. She didn't need to explain her behavior to him.

"Now you know how it feels, to have someone snooping around your private belongings. Prying and poking where they don't belong. It isn't very nice, is it?"

She put her hands on her hips, lifted her chin and waited to see how he'd respond. His eyes narrowed.

"So this is war. Is that what you're saying, Jennifer? No limits on either side?"

"Those are your rules, not mine."

Nick frowned. "I'm not the one who was spying in your bedroom."

"No. You're much too clever for such pedestrian tactics. You'd rather trick innocent people into giving you what you want."

Nick raised his gaze to the ceiling. She could see his jaw muscle twitching.

Jennifer used the momentary respite in their battle to cross the room and head for the doorway. She was in the wrong here. She knew that. If he hadn't shown up when he had, would she have gone so far as to pick up that report and read it?

Would she have crossed that line?

She didn't know the answer, and that troubled her.

"So what do you think?" Nick asked as she was about to leave.

She looked over her shoulder at him. "About what?"

He took her hand, pulled her back over the threshold and closed the door. "You read the report. I just want to know what you made of it."

Her gaze returned to the infamous

FedEx envelope. "I know that you ran a background check on Molly. I don't know what the report said."

Uncertainty flickered in his eyes. "You didn't read it?"

She was tempted to take the high moral ground of the falsely accused. But something inside her forced her to admit, "Only the cover letter."

Nick put his fingers under her chin. He held her face, his gaze steady on hers. "You really don't know then? I thought that was why you were so angry…"

"I don't have a clue." She glanced back at the report, still lying on the window seat cushion. She was almost unbearably curious about what that report said, but suddenly she was glad she hadn't stooped so low as to actually read it.

Despite her secrecy of the past few weeks, Molly was her friend. If she wanted Jennifer to know whatever was in that report, she would tell her.

Nick's eyes softened. "You're a good person, Jennifer March."

"People have a right to their privacy."

"People also have an obligation to be honest about the basics. Who they are, where they came from and what they're after. But perhaps you already know about Molly. Maybe I'm the fool here, making an issue out of something that everyone knows but me."

Frustrated, she pushed a hand against his chest and found it solid. Immovable. "Is this some sort of test?"

"Not at all. It just occurred to me that you might know. It's the sort of thing you *ought* to know, in my opinion."

Oh God, she couldn't take it anymore. What had he found out about Molly? "Well, I don't. I'm completely in the dark."

"Do you want me to fill you in?"

Jennifer wavered. She did. And she didn't. "Damn it, Nick," she said finally. "Life was *never* this complicated until you came to town."

CHAPTER FOURTEEN

JENNIFER DIDN'T WANT TO COAX the facts out of Nick. If he was right and the information in that report was something that Molly had been hiding from all of them, then she needed to get the truth straight from Molly.

"Will you please move, Nick? I'm going to talk to Molly."

"Good luck with that," he said, as he stepped to the side.

She let out a dry laugh. "Yeah. Exactly."

He touched her shoulder as she passed by. For a moment she paused, but he said nothing, just gave her a little smile.

"If you want to talk later, I'll be up here."

Right. Like they were friends or something. All he really wanted was for her to share the details of her conversation with Molly.

"See you later, Nick."

She ran down the stairs then went outside to the truck. As she turned left onto the main road, brilliant sunlight had her reaching for her sunglasses on the dash. Another spectacular September day. But how could she enjoy the weather when there was all this crazy stuff going on?

She didn't want to speculate about what that report had said about Molly. Neither did she want to think about the way she'd felt—the way her insides had turned to warm mush—when Nick had touched her.

So instead she thought about the forget-me-not song. For days she'd been wondering what her friends were going to say when they found out she'd actually written that chorus. Would they just be surprised? Or would they feel angry, even cheated?

How many times had she listened to them speculate about the one special friend, and not said a word. At times she'd even pretended to be as puzzled as they were.

After Simone's death there'd been times she'd been tempted to tell them the truth. But she'd realized that each of the guys, for their own reasons, had *needed* to believe that that song was for them. She hadn't wanted to take that away from them.

She wished she could convince Nick to keep the truth to himself, but she knew better than to think such a thing was possible. This was just the sort of twist that would make headlines...and sell thousands of copies of books.

It wouldn't be a huge story, the way Simone's death had been three years ago, and Emerson's one year later. Still, Jennifer had no doubt that at least a few journalists would want to talk to her to get an inside angle.

The prospect made her sick.

Spotting the yoga studio up ahead, Jennifer eased her foot off the gas. There were no other vehicles on the street, and Molly's car was in the driveway.

So far, so good.

She parked and went to the front door. A moment after she knocked she noticed the curtain at the window move a little.

Was Molly going to just ignore her?

Jennifer knocked louder this time. "Molly?" She was not going home without answers this time.

She was about to walk around to the back of the house and try the entrance off the kitchen, when finally the front door swung open.

Molly's face was flushed, and she looked harassed. For once she wasn't wearing yoga clothes, but capri jeans and a paint-splashed T-shirt. Cautiously, she glanced out at the street, then back at Jennifer.

"Are you alone?"

"Of course I'm alone. I don't usually travel with an entourage, do I?"

Molly's eyes widened and Jennifer realized that she'd startled her with her uncharacteristic anger. Well, she had reason to be angry, darn it. "Can I come in?"

"Nick Lancaster isn't with you, is he?"

"Why would he be?"

"He called and left a message. He said I had a day."

"A day to do what?" Then Jennifer understood. "To tell me who you really are, is that it, Molly?"

Molly glanced away and swallowed.

She looked so guilty that Jennifer felt a flicker of fear. Was she ready for the truth? She had to be. "Who are you? Why did you really come to Summer Island?"

Molly covered her face. "Damn that Nick."

"Molly..."

She grabbed Jennifer's arm. "Come inside. We can't discuss this on the street."

Jennifer allowed herself to be pulled into the living room. The room was tidy, but the adjoining dining room was a creative jumble at the moment. An easel sat in the center of the room. The table had been pushed to the side and was covered with a sheet of plastic. On the table were a glass jar of paintbrushes and about a dozen different tubes of paint. Light poured in from the south-facing windows, illuminating the portrait of a woman on the easel.

It was Simone.

Jennifer couldn't help staring. The picture wasn't a perfect likeness, but Molly had captured something. "I didn't know you were an artist."

"It's just a hobby." Molly made a dismissive gesture.

Jennifer tore her attention from the remarkable painting. "Nick says that when he was doing his research in New York, you were talking to the same people he was. That you were asking questions about Simone, too. You've been doing the same thing since you moved to the island. And it isn't a coincidence that you bought the house next to the Kincaids' vacation home either, is it?"

Molly crossed the room. She tightened

the lid on one of the tubes of paint, then sighed. "Yes, it's true. I moved here hoping to find out more about her. But I had good reason."

Jennifer waited.

"She was my sister."

Jennifer was stunned. She hadn't known what to expect, but she would never have guessed this. "But Simone was an only child."

"I'm not surprised that she thought that. But she *was* my older sister. Half sister to be exact." Molly settled her small, paint-splattered hands on her hips.

"This is so hard to believe."

"I felt the same way. That's why I had to find out everything I could about her. I felt so cheated. I would never get to meet her and talk to her. I'd never find out if we both hated brussel sprouts, yet loved broccoli. Never be able to compare the mole above my left ankle with hers—"

"The mole." Jennifer checked out Molly's bare ankle. There was the mole, just like Simone's. Somehow this small proof seemed more convincing than any-thing else.

She examined her friend closer, search-ing for other similarities, despite the dif-ferences in coloring. Simone had been dark-haired with peaches-and-cream skin, while Molly was a freckled redhead. Si-mone had been tall and willowy; Molly was petite and athletic looking.

Yet, the shape of the lips…the nose… Yes, there was a resemblance, if you looked hard enough.

"How did Nick find out?"

Jennifer couldn't see any reason to keep it secret. "He hired an investigator to perform a background check on you." She moved closer to the painting, tried to pin down the elusive quality of Simone's smile, but couldn't.

"Damn…" Molly ran a hand down the side of her ponytail. "This is so unfair."

"I don't like what Nick did either. But why have you been keeping this a secret? I thought we were friends. But I didn't even know who you were."

And she'd made such an effort to include Molly, to make her feel welcome on Summer Island. That was what hurt the most. She'd urged Harrison and Gabe and Aidan to be friendly, and now she'd discovered that Molly had deceived them all.

"I never *lied*."

"Semantics, Molly. When I think of all the questions you asked us about Simone. And we all thought you were just a fan."

"I am sorry about that. But I was so curious. How do you think you'd feel if you suddenly found out you had a half sister…and she happened to be one of the most famous musicians on the planet?"

"Why did you wait until Simone was dead to come to Summer Island?"

"I didn't know I was her sister until her death was reported in the papers. My mother was afraid to tell the truth."

"Your mother…" Jennifer swallowed. "Andrea DeRosier?"

Molly pointed at the canvas.

"Simone?" Jennifer didn't understand. And then suddenly she did. The portrait wasn't of Simone, but of her mother, Andrea.

Jennifer took a closer look. While the woman shared Simone's legendary beauty, Jenn could see now that she was older—in her forties or maybe even fifties. Simone hadn't been fortunate enough to live that long.

This woman's eyes were different, too. Though they were the same rich shade of brown as Simone's, their expression was almost unbearably melancholy.

"She was DeRosier," Molly added. "But she took my dad's name after their marriage."

"She remarried," Jennifer said dully. The woman they'd all assumed had to be dead had actually remarried and had a second daughter. A possibility occurred to her. "Is she still alive?"

Molly made a half turn away from her. Slender shoulders tightening, she admitted, "Yes. I'm sorry I lied about that."

"But why? Good God, why, Molly? We would have been so happy to meet

Simone's family. No one thought Simone's mother was still alive and of course we never dreamed she might have a sister." The secrecy just didn't make sense.

"I would have loved to be able to do that. But I couldn't. I made a promise."

"To your mother?"

Molly nodded. "She didn't want me to come to Summer Island at all. Turns out she was right to be worried. Now that Nick's found this out, my mother is going to be devastated."

"But why?" There was still so much Jennifer didn't understand. "Why did your mother leave Simone in the first place? And why didn't she tell you about your sister earlier?"

"This is my mother's story to tell, not mine." Molly went to the center of the living room, then wrapped her arms around her middle. She looked alone and vulnerable and Jennifer couldn't help but feel badly for her.

"What is your mother trying to hide?"

Molly shook her head. "I'm sorry. I can't tell you that."

Sorry. Was that all Molly had to say to her? Jennifer thought back to the conversation they'd had weeks ago when she'd shared her feelings about her own mother's death. She'd never told anyone else all that she'd told Molly that day. And in return Molly had *lied* to her. "This really sucks."

Molly touched her arm tentatively. "Jennifer, for what it's worth, I've enjoyed being your friend so much. And I wish things could have been different from the beginning."

She wasn't the only one.

Pushing aside her own hurt, Jennifer thought of Simone. "Do you have any idea how abandoned Simone felt after her mother left? How could a mother do that to her child? And why did she never contact her later? Her daughter was one of the most famous women in America. It wouldn't have been difficult to find her."

"My mother had her reasons, Jenn. You know I'd tell you if I could."

Jennifer shook her head in frustration. Molly's secretiveness made no sense. But then she remembered something else. "Is that why you volunteered to babysit Autumn a couple of summers ago? Because she's your niece?"

"I was desperate to get to know her," Molly admitted. "And to make sure she was all right."

"If you'd just told the truth—"

"I couldn't. Everything isn't always as black and white as we'd like it to be." She took a step back. "Would you stop looking at me like that? It's not as if I hurt anyone."

"That's debatable." If she had to describe how she felt right now, hurt would be right up there on the list. And she knew she wouldn't be the only one of her friends to feel this way. "Molly, what you've been doing is dishonest. It's wrong."

"I'm sorry you feel that way. But I didn't have a choice."

Did Molly really believe that?

"Jenn, you've got some pull with Nick, right? Is there any chance you could talk him into sitting on this? Why does the world need to know that Simone had a sister? It's not as if I was ever part of her life anyway."

Mad as she felt at Molly right now, Jennifer couldn't help sympathizing, just a little. It was one thing to have your secrets exposed to your friends. It was another to have them revealed to the world in a book.

"Molly, nothing I said to Nick would make a difference, trust me. If I had that sort of influence over the man, he would have left the island the day after he arrived here."

Molly sank into a chair, her face in her hands. "What am I going to do?"

"You don't have a choice. You've got to tell everyone who you really are. And if you're dating Gabe, like I think you are, then you'd better start with him." Jennifer straightened her shoulders. "Or I'll do it for you."

MOLLY WAS SIMONE'S SISTER. Jennifer could hardly focus for the rest of the day as she tried to absorb that fact. So many nights she and Simone had talked about how lonely it was to be an only child. They'd joked about becoming blood sisters, and one night they'd actually performed the finger-pricking ceremony that they'd read about.

Simone would have been *thrilled* to find out she had a real sister. Why had Andrea denied her daughters that happiness? It all came back to the one mystery that had eaten at Simone until her death…

Why had her mother deserted her?

Simone's pain resonated throughout so much of her music. Had her mother never listened to the songs? If so, hadn't she *heard* the plea in them?

True to his word, Nick stayed in his room and worked all day. Jennifer did not take him up on his offer to talk. Instead, after her evening chores she went to the office where she kept her CD collection and sat on the rug next to the cabinet.

During her career Simone had put out

seven CDs and Jennifer had all of them—personally signed—naturally. Simone had favored black-and-white photos for her cover shots, each one of a different body part, or facial feature. Jennifer took all seven CDs off the shelf and spread them over the cotton rug on the floor. She stared at them for a while, then began moving them, like pieces of a puzzle, trying to see how they fit best.

She arranged the facial features first: Simone's eye, a profile of her nose, her lips curved in a smile. The end result looked a little like a Picasso ink drawing.

Below the face, Jennifer put the photo of Simone's hand splayed over a piano keyboard, a shot taken from above of Simone's narrow foot in a sandal, the curve of Simone's neck from behind, and most daring of all, a photo of Simone's breast beneath the title, Within My Heart.

This was the CD Jennifer reached for first. She cracked open the case and pulled out the booklet with Simone's handwritten lyrics.

The third track was Simone's second Grammy-winning song, "Don't Leave Now." Widely interpreted as a romantic ballad from a woman to her lover, Jennifer had always suspected Simone had written it to her mother.

She slipped the CD into the player and turned the volume low. The opening chords set a mood of nostalgic longing, mingled with quiet sadness.

A movement in the doorway caught Jennifer's attention. Nick was standing there, watching her, his expression tender. He looked nothing like the sharp, exploitive writer she needed to see him as. She couldn't continue looking at him, without feeling something too big for her to handle right now. So she focused on the CD cover in her hands.

"That's one of my favorites," he said.

"Mine, too."

"Mind if I listen for a while?"

She hesitated, then nodded. He stepped into the room, closing the door behind him. He sat on the floor beside her and reached for the CD case. "'Don't Leave Now,' right?"

"Yes."

"I think she wrote this one for her mother."

He'd never met Simone and yet he knew. "I think so, too."

They listened for a few minutes, then Jennifer found herself blurting out, "I talked to Molly. She told me she was Simone's half sister."

Nick took a moment to absorb that. "Good. I'm glad you know."

"I'm still kind of stunned by it all. Most of us figured that Andrea had died shortly after she left her husband and Simone. But apparently she remarried and had another child."

"Yeah. I was pretty shocked, too."

"Molly should have told us this from the beginning. I still can't understand why she didn't."

"There must be a reason."

"She's trying to protect her mother.

From what, I don't know. Why does she even *want* to protect her? How can anyone condone a mother for doing what Andrea did? She abandoned her own daughter. And kept two sisters from ever knowing each other."

"We may never know what motivated Andrea to do those things. But one thing is clear. Her mother's desertion had a profound impact on Simone's music. Listen to this." Nick pointed to the lyrics printed on the CD insert. *"I sing in an empty room. You're not here, you're everywhere.* If that isn't about her mother, I don't know anything about Simone De-Rosier."

Jennifer shivered, then nodded. It was eerie, the way Nick had crawled into the skin of a woman he'd never even met.

"When we were kids, Simone used to talk about her mother all the time. She used to imagine her mother's reactions to everything she said or did."

Jennifer had felt so sorry for her. Her mother had been such a constant presence in her own childhood. So many of their family traditions had revolved around her.

Like afternoon tea. Every day when Jennifer came home from school she'd joined her parents in the kitchen for a feast of muffins or scones and fruit and a big pot of tea. As a child, Jennifer's tea had been mostly milk, but her mom had poured it into a real teacup and Jennifer had felt so grown up as she'd pinched the delicate handle between her thumb and forefinger.

The first time Jennifer had made tea for her father, after her mother's passing, the old tradition had seemed empty, almost painful. She'd gone through the usual rituals with the hope that one day the routine wouldn't be a struggle anymore.

But it had been so hard.

And she'd been an adult. How much more difficult it must have been for eleven-year-old Simone, who hadn't even been able to look to her coldhearted father for comfort. And not only had Simone had to deal with the loss of her mother, but also the fact that her mother had *decided* to leave.

"Nick, this is all so sad. When we were kids, Simone loved to pretend that we were sisters. I think she would have been thrilled to find out about Molly."

Nick didn't say anything. Jennifer glanced over at him and saw that he was watching her. He looked a little puzzled, but he was also smiling.

"You're a nice person, Jennifer March."

She didn't know what to say. She felt a blush coming on and ducked her head self-consciously. Clever repartee was in order, but she'd never been good at that sort of thing.

As the song they'd been listening to ended, Nick asked, "Mind if I put something else on?"

"Go ahead."

He picked an Aaron Lines CD, then jumped ahead to the track for "You Can't Hide Beautiful." Had he just chosen that song at random?

He reached out his hand and tucked

her hair behind her ear, his expression tender like it had been earlier, his touch even more so.

Was this just another of his cons? Jennifer didn't know what to think. He raised his arm in invitation and she shifted closer, letting his chest support most of her weight.

"Relax, Jenn. Just listen."

She closed her eyes and allowed the magic of the music to sink through her skin. She and Nick sat there through the entire CD, and slowly Jennifer became aware of something changing between them.

The spark she'd felt the first time she'd met him was stronger than ever. Even though she now knew who he was and what he was going to do, she'd never been more attracted to a man than she was to Nick.

Just a few days ago that knowledge had scared her.

But now, she shifted her head so she could look him in the eyes. And held her breath, wondering if he would do what she wanted him to do.

Kiss her.

NICK WAS BEING DRAWN TOWARD Jennifer as if by a force he couldn't understand or contain. He didn't know what was happening to him.

He was a man on a mission.

Yet this sweet, beautiful woman kept derailing him.

He lowered his head and let his mouth search out hers. She didn't turn away, didn't even hesitate. He felt her melt into the moment, wrapping her arms around his shoulders and kissing him back with uninhibited passion.

For a moment he pulled back, then pressed his face against her neck, inhaled her scent, relished her warmth.

He wanted her so badly, on so many levels. He wanted to make love with her, to confide in her, to hold her and never let go.

"Kiss me again, Nick."

Her words made his head spin. What man could ever say no to this woman? He touched his mouth gently to hers. Teased her, then breathed her in and claimed her.

His hands slid under her shirt, skimmed up her bare back. She felt deliciously warm and smooth. His fingers slipped under her bra strap, but before he could release the catch, she pulled away.

"Wait."

He was breathing hard. "You're killing me, Jennifer."

"I can't do this. We have to stop."

He brushed his lips over her ear. "Any chance you might change your mind?"

She closed her eyes tight. "No."

He sighed. He'd heard her answer, but the expression on her face wasn't the look of a woman who wanted a man to stop. Nevertheless, he forced his arms to his sides. "Is this about the book?"

"The book. And you. And me. The problem is none of those things mix." She sat up and pulled her shirt neatly into place. Nick, still sprawled on the office floor, felt like he'd been punched in the gut. He rolled onto his back and crossed his arms behind his head.

"Jenn, be reasonable. If I don't write it, someone else will. It's just a question of time."

"You've tried that argument on me before." Jennifer sighed, sounding weary. "But it isn't only the book I'm thinking of. You live in New York. You'll only be on the island another week. Right now I wish I was the sort of woman who could be happy with a casual affair, but I know I'm not."

"What I feel for you isn't casual."

He'd known from the first time he'd seen her that she was special. That she was pretty wasn't the point. There were plenty of pretty women more easily available than Jennifer.

Take that Emma at the library. She was single, very attractive and she'd made it clear she'd be happy to go out with him sometime, even though she was much younger than he was. Her stiff librarian persona was just the sort of challenge that normally appealed to him.

Yet, he hadn't acted on any of her hints. And wouldn't. Jenn was the woman he wanted. He couldn't get past that, no matter how hard he tried. Even now, after she'd turned him down, he wanted her.

And he had a strong suspicion she wanted him, too.

"Jenn, haven't you ever done something not because it was the smart thing to do but just because you wanted to?"

"Of course I have," she said, not sounding too confident.

"Well, then, what about us? Don't you think it would be worth a little risk for the chance to be together?"

He took her hands in his and tugged gently.

"Maybe it would be worth it in the short term," she said softly. "But that's not enough for me. Though it might be for you."

She lifted her gaze hesitantly to his, and

he understood what she was asking. He wanted her. But did he want her forever?

It was a fair question.

And he wasn't sure how to answer. He thought back over his past. He'd moved in with Karen shortly after his mother's remarriage. He'd gone from looking after his mom to taking responsibility for Karen and her child. As sad as he'd been when Karen had asked him to move out, a part of him had been relieved. He'd relished his newfound freedom, having never experienced it before. Since then he'd avoided any long-term commitment with the women in his life.

He'd written on his own schedule, traveled on a whim, indulged his need for company with casual, no-strings attached relationships.

Was he really willing to give up all that in order to be with Jenn? Because it wouldn't be fair for him to give less to her than she was prepared to give to him.

And Jenn was a girl who would lay her

entire heart and soul on the line. You just had to look into her eyes to see that.

Nick lowered his gaze to the floor. He wanted to take this woman upstairs to his bedroom...not do the honorable thing.

Shit.

"Maybe you're right, Jenn. You and me. Bad idea. But it sure felt good for a while there, didn't it?" He pulled himself up from the floor then reached out for her hands. But she was already standing, already on her way out of the room.

When she said good night, she didn't look him in the eyes, and he realized that sometimes, no matter what they said, honesty simply did not pay.

CHAPTER FIFTEEN

ON SUNDAY ALL THE B and B guests except Nick checked out, so the next morning Jennifer prepared a small strawberry frittata for breakfast. She baked the egg mixture in her mother's old cast-iron frying pan, then cut it into wedges and placed the pan at the center of the table for her dad, aunt and Nick to help themselves.

Nick came down late and ate quickly before leaving for the day. Her father seemed oblivious to how fastidiously they avoided each other's eyes, but Jennifer's aunt gave her a sharp glance.

Don't ask, Jennifer pleaded silently as Annie stepped into the kitchen to help with the dishes.

"Is everything okay, Jennifer?"

"Fine." Jennifer hand washed the large serving platter she'd used for the toasted day-old cinnamon buns. Annie picked up a towel to dry. Her knuckles were swollen from her arthritis and Jennifer could tell it caused her pain to help even with such a simple chore. "Please leave it," she said to her aunt.

"You do so much for your father and me. But I hope you know that we would never want to stand in the way of your happiness."

"You don't."

"You're always thinking of others and that's a good thing, but you're a young woman. Your father and I have had a chance to live our lives. Just as your friends are doing, too. And sometimes I worry—"

Jennifer set down the dishcloth. "Annie, you and Dad are my family. This bed-and-breakfast is my home. And I wouldn't want things any other way."

It wasn't totally true. There were times when Jennifer did long for her freedom.

Times when she wished she could hop on a plane and fly far, far away.

But her life had never accommodated choices like that. At least not since her mother died.

Annie smiled and Jennifer thought that her answer had satisfied her. But a moment later, Annie said, "That Nick Lancaster seems like a nice man. The two of you were in the office together for quite a while last night."

Jennifer pulled the plug from the sink and watched the water begin to drain. "We were listening to music."

Annie gave her another of her sharp looks. Her hands might be arthritic, but there was nothing wrong with her mind or her powers of observation. "Did you argue?"

"Not really." Jennifer dried her hands, then reached for the grocery list next to the phone. "I'm going to town this morning. Is there anything I can get for you?"

Annie thought for a moment. "Could you return a couple of library books for me? Wait a minute and I'll go get them."

She left the room before Jennifer had a chance to say anything else, but Jennifer wasn't fooled.

Obviously her aunt knew where Nick was spending his days, too.

AFTER A TRIP TO THE POST office, the bank and the grocery store, Jennifer decided to stop in at Derby's Diner for a cup of coffee and a piece of pie. She was surprised to find Harrison and Gabe sitting opposite one another in a booth near the back.

Jennifer could remember the days when seeing one dark head and one blond head bowed together meant something fun was in the works. Now she worried quite the opposite was afoot. She made her way to the back of the diner in time to hear Gabe, whose back was toward her, say, "—getting my dad's boat out of storage. See if she's still seaworthy. Interested?"

"Hell, yeah. That Flying Dutchman was the fastest thing I've ever sailed." Harrison noticed her then. "Jennifer."

"Hi, guys." She looked from face to face, trying to figure out what was going on.

"Have you got a minute, Jenn? Sit down," Gabe invited.

Harrison slid over to make room on the bench seat. "We were just talking about Gabe's father's old boat. Do you remember it?"

"Sure." She'd never been a fan of sailing, but she'd enjoyed watching the guys from the patio at the marina. "Are you two actually going to sail together?"

"If the old boat is up to it." Gabe spoke as if their plans were no big deal, but Jennifer knew they were. Finally, finally, these two were talking again.

A passing server noticed Jennifer's arrival and poured her a coffee. "Would you like anything else?"

Jennifer was debating over which pie to choose, when Nessa entered the diner with Dex and Tyler. She spotted Jennifer sitting next to her brother, and waved. "Hi! We have good news!"

It wasn't until she drew closer that Nessa realized her ex-husband was at the booth, too. As soon as she did, she stopped. Behind her, Dex put a steadying hand on her shoulder.

"Sorry," Nessa said. "I shouldn't be barging in."

Jennifer couldn't blame her for being surprised at seeing Harrison and Gabe in the same booth at Derby's Diner.

"That's fine," Gabe said smoothly. "It's nice to see you, Nessa. Dex." He smiled at seven-year-old Tyler. "I was just about to leave…" He started sliding across the vinyl seat.

"Hey, don't you want to hear our good news?" Tyler asked, hopping from one foot to the other. "I'm going to have a baby sister!"

Gabe's face fell. His gaze went to Nessa's flat stomach, then quickly away.

Jennifer noted Gabe's painful reaction, even as she felt a confused mixture of pleasure and bewilderment. Nessa and Dex loved kids, but hadn't Nessa said she didn't want to risk aggravating her multiple sclerosis by getting pregnant?

Harrison, too, had been shocked into silence by Tyler's announcement. He stared mutely from his sister to Dex.

"I'm not pregnant," Nessa said in a rush. "We're adopting. Carolyne is one week old. Tomorrow we're going to Vancouver to bring her home."

Gabe was the first to react to the announcement. "I'm happy for you, Nessa."

If he was, he certainly didn't look it. Still, Jennifer gave him an A for effort as he turned his sad eyes to Dex and said, "Congratulations. I wish you the very best."

Jennifer knew she wasn't the only one who could tell what a huge effort those words cost Gabe.

He left then, exiting through the main doors. From the window Jennifer could see him walking with his shoulders slumped, hands shoved into the pockets of his pants. He looked very alone as he made his way across the street toward his office.

"Excuse me? Gabe?" Molly ran along the sidewalk, cursing the heels on her sandals.

"Molly?" Gabe had left the diner looking like he'd been eviscerated, but now, a small smile softened his expression.

She took heart from that subtle sign that he was glad to see her. "I was in the café." She gasped for another breath. "I heard what Tyler said."

She'd been sitting in the corner, tucked out of sight in case Nick Lancaster happened by. God, she was tired of hiding from that man.

"Tyler sure was excited, wasn't he?"

Gabe sounded mildly amused, but Molly wasn't fooled. He'd been shattered by his ex-wife's announcement. Molly had an urge to kiss him, but she knew she couldn't.

Just last night he'd called her and suggested a picnic on Pebble Beach after dark. They'd had a wonderful time and Molly had been so happy...as long as she kept her worries about Nick Lancaster and yesterday's conversation with Jennifer out of her mind.

She was almost out of time. In a matter of days, maybe even less, Jennifer would spread the word among the forget-me-not friends. Gabe would find out who she really was and he'd be furious.

It was a reaction she couldn't stand to see. She had to be gone before he found out.

But oh, it was hard, so very hard, to contemplate leaving.

Though she wanted to kiss him, she compromised by squeezing his arm. "Yes, it's happy news for Nessa and Dex. But what about you, Gabe?"

"I'm glad for Nessa, but you're right, I felt a little envious as well. I always assumed that when Nessa had kids, I'd be the dad."

Even though she had no right, Molly felt a painful twist of jealousy.

"Still," he went on, "Nessa and I have

been divorced for a while so I guess it was just a knee-jerk reaction."

He looked at her intently and his eyes were so blue and clear that Molly couldn't focus on anything else.

"So, what brings you to town today, Molly?"

"Just errands. I was going to pop by your office and see if we'd had any offers." She'd take anything now. She didn't care what price. She just had to get off this island before she fell completely apart.

"We had one this morning," Gabe said. "But it's still too low in my opinion. I say we hold out for at least five thousand more. Or…better yet, let's just take your house off the market."

He took her arm and led her around the corner to a recessed doorway. Pulling her in close, he kissed her. Thoroughly. Possessively. The way she'd been wanting to kiss him since she first saw him at the diner.

"Why do you have to move when I want you to stay so badly?"

She felt the exact same way. If only she could say so. "We haven't been dating for very long."

"No. But it's been an incredible couple of weeks. Hasn't it?"

"Yes." He looked at her so hopefully. "I mean no." She shook her head. "I don't know what I mean, only that I can't stay, Gabe, I can't."

She thought about the hours they'd spent kissing and talking the other night. No, she didn't want to leave. If only she had some other choice...

From across the street, a flash of blue caught her eye. It was a man in a brightly colored shirt. He noticed her at the same instant she saw him. He stopped in his tracks, and instead of carrying on in the direction of the library, started her way.

It was Nick Lancaster.

"I don't care if the offer is less than expected," she told Gabe. "I want to accept it. I'll come by your office tomorrow to sign whatever papers are necessary."

Gabe withdrew. He looked so hurt, but

there was nothing she could do. When he found out the truth about her, he'd be glad then.

One quick check around the corner told her that Nick was being held up from crossing the street by a farmer in a pickup truck. Fortunately her car was nearby, parked in front of the bakery.

She sprinted for it, then drove away without another glance at the men behind her.

JENNIFER DECIDED TO HAVE a slice of pie after all. She enjoyed the sweet fruit and flaky pastry as she listened to Nessa and Harrison plan a welcome home party for baby Carolyne. Jennifer couldn't help wondering about Gabe. Would he ever remarry, maybe have a family of his own?

Later, as she walked along the street to the library, Jennifer realized that her friends probably wondered the same thing about her.

She thought of Nick. If only they had met under different circumstances. Maybe if she weren't tied to Summer Island and he weren't writing that book…

Jennifer stopped at her parked truck to get her aunt's books. It seemed Annie's attempt at matchmaking was going to fail. For once Nick's Rover wasn't in front of the library. Jennifer made her way inside the quiet building and found Emma Parks at the front desk, reading. She put her book aside and smiled at Jennifer.

"I haven't seen you in here all summer. I have a new Joy Fielding hardcover for you."

"Really?" Jennifer hadn't put up her feet and settled in with a good book since last winter. "I'm not sure if I dare borrow it, Emma. I can never start one of her books and not finish it a day or two later. And I'm so busy right now."

She dumped her aunt's books into the return bin, then paused for a closer look at Emma. As usual the young woman was dressed to downplay her rather lush figure and pretty features. "How have you been?"

"Oh, I'm fine. I've been busy, too,

helping that writer who's been staying at your place. Isn't he wonderful?" Emma held up the book she'd been reading so Jennifer could see the cover. It was Nick's latest.

Jennifer had an odd desire to rip it out of her hands. She immediately mocked herself for her jealous reaction. Emma was pretty, but she was only just twenty. Surely much too young to be of interest to Nick.

"He's a fascinating guy, all right. So Nick's been spending a lot of time at the library?" Jennifer noticed a stack of old movie magazines on a trolley next to the desk. "Did he request these?"

"Yes. I made copies of the stories about Simone for him."

When Jennifer looked at her again, surprised, Emma blushed. "It's often not that busy in here. I've enjoyed helping."

Oh, really? Jennifer stifled a smile as she went to check out the magazines. Who was she to fault Emma for a reaction that she could understand all too well.

She leafed through the magazines until she saw one that looked uncomfortably familiar. Simone was on the cover. Over the years Simone had been on the cover of many magazines, but wasn't this the one where…

Checking the publication date, a feeling of unease crept over her. She turned to a page marked by a pink sticky note and though she should have expected it, felt a jolt at the sight of Simone posing on the arm of Jennifer's former fiancé, Barry Collins.

She'd seen this picture before, too, ages ago, back when she'd been engaged. She could remember the moment she'd first laid eyes on it. She'd been at the hairdressers, waiting her turn at the shampoo sink, when Phyllis had tossed the magazine at her.

"This came in the mail today. Latest issue. Tell us what that girl has been up to this month."

Obligingly, Jennifer had flipped to the article on Simone. And when she'd seen

that picture of her fiancé with her best
friend, she'd understood what the expression *sucker punched* was all about.

That night Simone had called to see if
she'd picked up the latest issue of *People*.
She'd told Jennifer not to be alarmed.
Harrison had been out of town and Barry
had offered to be her escort to a movie
opening, that was all.

Jennifer had said, sure, she understood,
everything was fine.

But of course, it hadn't been. Barry
should have told her, even if it was just an
innocent outing, he definitely should have
told her. The fact that Jennifer couldn't be
one hundred percent certain it *had* been
just an innocent outing tipped the scales.
She'd broken off their engagement shortly
thereafter, and Simone had flown back to
Summer Island, full of apologies.

"Nothing happened between us, Jennifer. You have to believe me."

And Jennifer did believe her. Sort of.
She knew Simone and Harrison had an
agreement about these situations. Simone

hated going to functions alone and Harrison was often out of town on business.

But their arrangement worked because they were honest with one another. And Barry hadn't been with her.

"It wasn't her fault," Jennifer repeated softly as she gazed, transfixed, at the airbrushed perfection of Simone's face.

Years ago, when Jennifer had been dealt this blow, all her anger had been focused on Barry. But she'd handled that betrayal. Now she found herself wondering something she hadn't thought much about at the time.

Why had Simone asked Jennifer's fiancé to be her escort that night? She could have had her pick from many other men. Her agent, for instance, had often accompanied her on professional outings when Harrison wasn't available.

Why had Simone selected Barry?

A shadow fell over the magazine and Jennifer looked up. Nick was in front of her, looking concerned.

"That's him, isn't it?" he asked. "The guy you were engaged to?"

She hesitated, then nodded.

"When you mentioned his name, I was sure I'd heard it before. It took me a while to remember where and when."

He'd seen this picture before, then. Jennifer wondered what else he'd uncovered about Barry and Simone. Then decided she didn't want to know. She closed the magazine and replaced it carefully on the stack with the others.

Nick followed her as she left the library. She paused when they reached the sidewalk.

"Are you okay?" he asked.

"Sure." She wondered if she'd always known the truth and just not wanted to admit it. At any rate, the answer was crystal clear to her now.

The reason Simone had asked Barry to take her to the premiere was because she couldn't stand the fact that there was a man in the world who actually preferred Jennifer to her.

It hadn't been enough for Simone that she had millions of adoring fans. Or that Harrison, Gabe and Emerson all adored her. No, she'd had to add Barry to the list of her men, even though she'd been the one to introduce him to Jennifer in the first place.

"She didn't care about me at all. My feelings didn't even enter the equation."

"What, Jennifer? Are you talking about Simone?"

She couldn't answer. Her throat had unaccountably backed up and she couldn't say a word. Nick put a hand on her lower back and led her to the bench at the side of the building.

She let him pull her to the seat, but she couldn't look at him. She was concentrating all her energy on holding back the tears. She didn't want to break down in such a public place. Especially not in front of Nick. She pulled in a deep breath, using the technique Molly had taught her for yoga.

Nick squeezed her shoulder. "I'm sure she didn't realize how much she hurt you."

He'd figured it all out, too. Knew exactly what she'd been talking about. "How can you say that?"

"Because it's clear that she cared about you. I figured that out the first day I was on the island, when I saw those photographs on your fridge."

"Yeah, me and my best friend. Some best friend." Tears were leaking out the corners of her eyes and she gritted her teeth.

Self-absorption had been part of the package that was Simone. Jennifer had accepted that fact. But maybe she'd been too accepting of it.

"Nick, thanks for being so understanding. But I need to get back to the B and B. Teatime, you know." She managed a trembling smile.

"I'm sure your father would understand if you skipped it this once."

"No, really, I'm fine."

He brushed a tear from her cheek with his thumb. "I could drive you if you like."

She slipped out from under his arm.

"No, you go ahead with your work." He'd surely been going to the library for a reason. "I'll see you later."

She left with her head high, confident in her ability to hold herself together. Dry eyes were necessary when you were seeing your friends clearly for the very first time.

CHAPTER SIXTEEN

As soon as she was in the truck, Jennifer realized Nick had been right to question her ability to drive. Her fingers were trembling so much she had trouble fitting the key into the ignition.

She took it slow as she pulled out from the parking space and headed down the island road. Painful memories—long shoved to the back of her mind—came back to mock her. Her final visit to L.A. Returning her engagement ring to Barry and the way he couldn't even look her in the eye.

Then back home more fun had awaited. Canceling the church and the hall for the wedding. Returning her dress. Phoning all the guests to tell them about the change in plans.

She'd had to deal with all of that. And Simone's contribution? A huge bouquet of pink roses and a note of apology.

But had she really been sorry? Sending flowers was easy if you had money. Just one phone call was all it took. And most likely the call had been made by Simone's assistant, not her.

What Jennifer had really needed back then was someone to talk to, a shoulder to cry on. Her other friends had been there for her, but not Simone.

Yes, Simone was busy, but surely she could have made a little time in her schedule if she'd thought it was important. Most likely she hadn't given Jennifer's feelings a thought, just as it had probably never occurred to her to give Jennifer any credit for the lyrics in the forget-me-not song.

That's all Jennifer would have wanted. She didn't care about the money.

She could remember receiving Simone's first CD in the mail. Simone had had a copy delivered to her. Jennifer had torn off the wrappings and eagerly read every word in the jacket, secretly hoping to find some form of acknowledgment.

But there'd been nothing.

Jennifer couldn't help but think of all the times Simone had told her she loved her like a sister. If that really was the case, then maybe Molly was lucky she'd never had a chance to get to know Simone when she was alive.

Molly... Seeing the yoga studio ahead, Jennifer ground her teeth together. There was another supposed friend who'd been anything but. All this time they'd been hanging out together and Molly had never told her the truth about who she was and why she'd moved to the island.

Molly. Simone. They were more alike than she had first realized.

As Jennifer sped past the yoga studio, she noticed Gabe's car in the driveway. He was putting a Sold sticker over the For Sale sign.

So Molly really was serious about leaving the island.

Well, *good*. Jennifer was glad.

At home Jennifer prepared tea as usual, setting out the food on the table for her father and aunt and the few guests who had checked in that afternoon.

When she was done, she went to the back door and shoved her feet into her gardening clogs. Her father looked up from the table. "Aren't you joining us?"

"Not today, Dad. I ate in town. Besides, I have work to do in the barn."

Not yet ready to be around people, she stayed in the barn for several hours. By the time she returned to the kitchen, the leftover food had been put away, the counters were spotless and her aunt was drying her hands at the sink.

She knew her foul mood was obvious and she was grateful that Annie didn't say anything about it.

"Do we have any empty boxes?" she asked.

"There's an old apple box in the closet."

"Thanks." Jennifer dug it out, then went to the fridge and started pulling down the postcards and mementos tacked to the board.

"It's good to houseclean every now and then," her aunt said. She patted Jennifer's shoulder on her way out of the room.

Jennifer took down every picture, every postcard. With each one came a flood of memories that she no longer wanted to acknowledge. For years she'd been determined to see only the good in her friends. Now she felt as if she could see nothing but the bad.

A faint noise in the background gradually became louder. Jennifer tensed as she recognized the distinctive engine noise of Nick's Rover pulling up to the house.

Nick. She hadn't thought of him since she'd seen that photograph of Simone and Barry. Now she wondered what he was going to make of that in his book. Would he tell the world how Simone DeRosier had betrayed her?

Her stomach roiled at the thought and she pulled the next photo off the board so quickly the tack went flying across the floor. As she chased after it, she heard the front door open, then close. A moment later Nick appeared in the kitchen doorway.

She punched the tack back into the board, trying to avoid looking at him.

"Hey, you," he said gently. "Are you okay?"

"Sure." Damn, her voice had wobbled. She glanced at him to see if he'd noticed. He looked glad to see her and worried all at the same time.

She turned away, swallowing a welling of emotion that she couldn't name.

"What's going on?" His gaze dropped to the box at her feet. He stepped closer and saw the empty bulletin board. "Jenn?"

She crossed her arms over her chest and leaned against the fridge. It would be stupid to cry. She was just doing something she should have done years ago. Every one of the forget-me-not friends had moved on since the old days. They'd gotten married, pursued careers, had children.

Everyone but her.

She'd stayed here at her parents' B and B, filling her days with dreams and memories of the past.

She shouldn't be angry at her friends, she realized suddenly, but at herself. It was her own fear of moving forward that had trapped her. Nothing else.

Recently Nick had asked her why she hadn't gone on any trips since Simone's death. Well, why hadn't she? It wasn't that difficult to hire extra help for the B and B, to book plane tickets and plan an itinerary.

Likewise, she'd used her failed engagement to Barry as an excuse to opt out of the dating scene. She could have made more of an effort to meet new people, *men* in particular.

And she definitely could have been more proactive about her career. Rather than shipping all her product to Saltspring, she could have opened her own shop, taken a few risks, expanded her horizons.

She'd been a coward, avoiding risk and heartbreak, but also fun and excitement.

And what better example of her timidness than the way she'd treated Nick? Every time he'd shown a little interest in her she'd pushed him away. She could have had one of the most romantic and exciting months of her life.

Instead, he'd be leaving in a matter of days and all she'd have to remember was a couple of kisses and a lot of what-ifs.

"Jennifer, I'm sorry." Nick came close enough to touch a strand of her hair. He let it slip between two fingers, while he continued to regard her with a concern that seemed almost loving.

She supposed it was kind of him to spare any thought to her feelings, when he'd just been handed another scoop for his biography. Booking into Lavender Farm B and B had certainly proven to be a wise move on his part. He now had everything he'd come to Summer Island to learn. And then some.

"I really *am* sorry," he said again, touching a finger to her chin and gently raising her head.

"There's nothing to be sorry about. I've decided I'm glad you're writing this book. You can't move on from your past, until you've accepted it. I didn't understand that until today."

"Wow. This is quite a turnaround." He looked at her uncertainly.

"It's overdue. No one else was as against this book as I was—certainly not my dad and aunt, or even Nessa and Harrison. I was the one with the problem and now I understand why. It wasn't that I didn't want the world to see the real Simone. *I* didn't want to see the real Simone."

"We don't have to talk about this right now. I know you're upset."

"But I want to talk about it. And I want you to know that you were right. I did put Simone on a pedestal. And as a result I treated my past as if it was more important than my future. Well, I'm done with that. It's time to move forward. And I want to start by looking ahead, not behind."

She would fill this bulletin board with

pictures of the places she wanted to visit, ideas for products to create, dreams for the future, not a shrine to the past.

"It's good to look ahead. But that doesn't mean you have to wash your hands of what has gone before."

"Actually, for right now, I think it does. I've got other stories you might want to use for your book, Nick. All you have to do is ask."

He looked tempted. Then he shook his head. "Maybe, Jenn. Let's discuss it later, okay?"

Why wasn't he jumping on her offer? Since the first day he arrived at the B and B he'd been trying to get her to talk about Simone. She looked in his eyes and thought about the other thing she'd noticed in him since the first time they met.

Did he still feel it, too? Was he still interested in her as a woman?

He stared right back at her, and heat washed over her body. She didn't need him to say a word to understand what he was feeling.

Yes. He was interested.

"Jenn." Nick put his hands on her shoulders. Eyes still locked together, they leaned toward one another.

And kissed.

Jenn had the shifting sensation again. Sand was slipping out from beneath her feet, even though she stood on solid ground. What was happening to her? Why did he make her feel this way…lost and found all at the same time.

He said her name again, pressing the word along with a kiss against her throat. "Let's go to my room," he said urgently.

She wanted to say yes. Wanted to go on kissing him, touching and exploring him, and having him do the same to her.

At the same time, a cold sensation curled around her heart. *Be careful. He's going to hurt you. He told you where you stood the other night. This isn't going anywhere. He's a successful author, from New York City and you're only—*

No. She wasn't going to think that way. She didn't care that Nick wasn't into forever. Now that the book was no longer between them, all that stood in the way was her own fear.

For years, she'd been the timid one, never demanding the spotlight. Well, today she wanted it. She wanted Nick's total, undivided attention.

It was time to embrace life, not hide from it.

"Not here. Pebble Beach," she murmured. "I'll grab a blanket from the closet. Do you have any more of that wine?"

AS NICK SLID BEHIND THE wheel of the Rover, he felt as nervous and keyed up as a kid on his first date. Beside him Jennifer seemed excited, too. She was cuddled as close to him as the seats would allow. He could smell the lavender in her hair, feel the warmth of her breath. Her hand rested near his knee and every time one of her fingers shifted, even if only by a mere fraction of an inch, he felt it. Man, did he feel it.

"Why are we prolonging this?" he asked, not really minding, just curious.

"I don't want to be the same old dull Jennifer. Pebble Beach will be more romantic. And this late in the season it should be deserted."

"It better be," he growled. Keeping one hand on the wheel, he rested the other over her hand. She inched a little closer, and he had to force himself to keep his eyes on the road.

A country love ballad came on the radio and Jennifer cranked the sound up high. Nick had never been a fan of country music until that moment.

It was growing dark by the time they pulled up to the beach. There was one other vehicle in the parking lot. He could see the couple and their small child splashing in the waves at the shore.

He and Jennifer headed away from them, to the secluded alcove where they'd sat before. He spread out the blanket, then opened the wine.

The wind was calm, the sky was clear.

It was a perfect night to sit and listen to the surf and breathe in the fresh sea air.

He couldn't believe he had her here with him. The issues with his book had been laid to rest. He had what he'd come here for. His editor and agent were going to salivate when they found out the truth behind the forget-me-not song.

And he'd found out about Simone's mother, too. That was another huge break he hadn't expected to get. He was going to hand in the most complete, the most authoritative biography that he could ever have dreamed of.

And the person he had to thank for this—most of it anyway—was now lying in his arms. Her skirt had ridden up to midthigh, revealing the long, sexy legs he'd imagined in his dreams for almost a month now.

He ran a hand along her smooth, warm skin and watched her eyes half close as a result.

"I love the way you touch me."

She couldn't have said anything that would have turned him on more. He searched out her mouth with his, and kissed her the way he'd wanted to in the kitchen earlier.

Like a man who had only one thought in his head.

Making love to this woman.

He caressed her leg, moving up to her hip bone, pooling her skirt at her waist. It was too dark to see the color of her panties, but they felt silky as he cupped her behind, then squeezed.

She splayed a hand over his chest, then slipped it across his back, down to his jeans. He let her pull him close to her, felt her shudder as their bodies connected as intimately as the fabric of their clothes would allow.

He'd planned on talking first. He'd thought there were some things that still needed to be discussed.

Like the fact that he would be leaving on Saturday...

But Jenn didn't seem to have any interest in words and if she didn't, then by God, neither did he. Shifting to a sitting position, he slipped his hands under her tank top and tugged it over her head. Her smooth bra went next, then his shirt.

He pulled her down to the blanket and kissed her some more. His hands teased her breasts. The tight hard buds of her nipples made him ache with need. He lowered his head for a taste and she moaned so sweetly he almost lost it.

Aside from the sweep of stars, it was pitch-dark outside. No moon. The couple with the kid had left a while ago and they were completely alone.

He found the button of her skirt and released her from the light, gauzy fabric.

"Your jeans, Nick," she said, her fingers at the stiff waistband.

It was too dark for her to see anything, so she used her hands. He shuddered as she ran both of them over his length, back and forth, then back to his butt and down his thighs.

He still closed his eyes as the pleasure pulsed over him. "I've dreamed of this from the first day I saw you."

"I guess I read your thoughts right then," she teased.

He kissed her again, and the magic and sweetness was just like the first time he'd kissed her in Arbutus Park. When he pulled her closer, when he ran his hands down her back, she seemed to melt against him.

"I want to make love to you."

"Yes, Nick."

"Are you sure?"

She tucked her face under his chin. "Yes," she whispered. The air from her mouth sent shivers over his skin.

It only took a few seconds to sheath himself, and as he reached for her again he couldn't imagine a better place to make love than at the foot of the Pacific Ocean, under a blanket of stars.

This is perfect. He slipped inside her. *Perfect.*

At her gasp, he froze. "Jenn?"

"Yes."

He couldn't tell anything from that one breathless word. "Second thoughts?"

"Oh, Nick. Definitely not." She arched against him, and instinct took over. Everything felt so right…so perfect.

In the back of his mind, though, almost buried under the intense pleasure of the moment, the voice of his guilt wouldn't be silenced.

This is great, but you're headed for trouble.

He didn't want to listen.

She's bruised. She's going to be hurt later. You're taking advantage of her.

He wasn't going to listen.

Lost to the rhythm of what they'd started together, he shut down his mind and concentrated on feelings. His and hers. He waited for her and then he followed, tumbling from heaven to sand in a spiral of pleasure.

In the quiet after, he could hear only the surf and the sound of her breath in his ear.

And the return of the voice he'd worked so hard to silence earlier.

Mistake.

He'd known better than to immediately accept her stamp of approval for his book.

Why hadn't he been strong enough to wait for this, too?

CHAPTER SEVENTEEN

THOUGH GABE DIDN'T USUALLY work in the real estate office until after lunch, he'd agreed to meet Molly there first thing Tuesday morning. Normally she taught three classes before noon, but today she put up a closed sign on the door to her yoga studio.

She felt terrible for all her clients who would show up only to be disappointed, but her time here on Summer Island had sadly run out.

Her talk with Jennifer had confirmed as much.

And now she had to deal with Gabe.

She showed up at the offices of Summer Island Realty five minutes before the arranged time. Flora wasn't in yet, and Gabe met her in the reception area.

There were a few seconds when neither one of them spoke. Then Gabe said, "Come on in."

She sat across the desk from him, almost choked by the angry vibrations in the room. She'd never seen Gabe's eyes this icy. Or his mouth so hard. Her gaze dropped to the contract on his otherwise empty desk.

"Is that it? The offer?"

He nodded. "Like I told you yesterday, I'm sure we could get a better price if we were patient."

She shook her head. "No. I want to get this settled."

Gabe's jaw muscles visibly tightened. "Your mind is made up, isn't it? You must be really anxious to get out of here."

"Not really. But I don't have a choice."

"Right." He spoke sarcastically, as he pushed the contract toward her.

She glanced over it, then signed quickly, before she could lose her nerve. When it was done, she set down the pen and swallowed. "There's something I should tell you."

Gabe looked like he wanted to tell her to go to hell, but he didn't actually say the words. Instead he glared at her and waited.

"If I don't tell you now, you'll hear from someone else. Probably Jennifer, or one of her friends. And I think it would be better coming from me."

When she paused for breath, he stayed silent. Only the blink of his eyes betrayed any curiosity on his part.

"You see, I haven't been completely honest about who I am and why I came to Summer Island."

The curiosity in his eyes turned to concern. She definitely had his interest now, that was for sure.

"I'm Simone's sister, Gabe. Her half sister, actually."

JENNIFER WOKE UP ALONE. Nick had wanted to sleep together, but she'd been reluctant. Not just because she didn't want to raise questions with her father and her aunt. She didn't want to have the memory of Nick in her bed because it would make it so much harder to forget him once he left.

Besides, though the idea of sleeping in Nick's arms sounded like heaven, in a way she was glad for the time alone. She wanted to savor the memory of their evening together. And come to terms with a new realization.

She was in love with Nick Lancaster.

It wasn't a crush, like what she'd felt for Gabe.

And she wasn't in love with love, the way she'd been when she'd accepted Barry's proposal.

No, this was real love. And it was wonderful because Nick was incredible and she'd never met anyone like him. But it was also terrible, because it was already Tuesday and Nick was planning to leave on Saturday.

She knew better than to hope that what had happened between them would change his plans. Last night he'd told her that his book was due in New York by the end of next week and that he wanted to deliver it to his agent in person.

With a heavy sigh, Jennifer got out of bed and started her morning routine. Shower, dress, then downstairs to prepare breakfast. Happiness burst through her when she saw Nick filling the coffee machine.

"You're up early." She'd planned to play it cool but it was impossible for her not to smile at him.

He glanced at her father who was in the kitchen, too, then gave her a wink. "I'm catching on to this early bird thing."

"Scrambled eggs this morning, Jennifer?" her father asked, oblivious to the interplay between them.

"Good idea, Dad." She grabbed the eggs from the fridge, then got out fruit for smoothies. Nick picked up a knife and helped her with the chopping.

He fits in so perfectly, she thought. He had from day one. How strange that a

New Yorker should have transplanted so easily. But she had to remember...this was only temporary.

She cracked ten eggs into a bowl, then added cold water and salt. "Where's the pepper?"

"Here." Her dad handed her the grinder. "I just refilled this."

She gave the grinder several hard twists before she realized something didn't smell right. She bent over the bowl of eggs and inhaled.

"Oh, no."

She examined the grinder under better light. Her father had refilled it all right. But instead of peppercorns he'd used whole cloves. Enough to make a hundred pumpkin pies.

"Dad, could you get the clean table napkins from the dryer, please?"

As soon as he was out of the room, she invited Nick to smell the pepper. He laughed and shook his head. "Are the eggs ruined?"

She dumped the mess down the sink.

"Fortunately, we have lots more. Poor Dad. He means well, but..."

"Hey, it was an honest mistake. Either of us could have made it."

Jennifer appreciated the way Nick stood up for her dad. And yet the incident felt more significant to her. It was a reminder that her father and her aunt needed her.

Nick had to go to New York.

She had to stay here.

Not even for a day could she indulge in a dream that there was any future for the two of them.

AFTER BREAKFAST, NICK WENT back to his room to finish writing. The words were really flowing now. There was so much to say. While he'd helped Jennifer clean up after breakfast, she'd shared some of her lighthearted stories of Simone and he wanted to get them down on paper before he forgot.

After a few hours, the words finally dried up. He stared out the window and wondered why he didn't feel better about his book right now.

It was terrific. More than he'd hoped for. Not only accurate and complete but also, he was pretty sure, a real page-turner. It could turn out to be his best seller after all.

And yet...he didn't feel right about it.

The problem was Jennifer, of course. She'd experienced a complete change of heart about this book. Or so it seemed. Nick couldn't help but think that she was going to change her mind.

One day, when she'd gotten around to forgiving Simone for the past—and she would forgive Simone, it wouldn't be in her nature to do otherwise—would she regret having assisted him with this project?

Would she look back on this time with loathing?

Feel like she'd been used and betrayed yet again?

Nick pushed out of his chair and went to stand by the window. His discomfort was growing stronger. He wanted to ignore it, go back to working on his book, forget the question of ethics and moral responsibility.

Damn it, he'd done nothing wrong. This was a good book and Jennifer *wanted* him to publish it.

That was what he believed, it really was, and yet his emotions were sending a different message. He tried desperately to ignore the message, and yet, as minutes went by and then an hour, the feeling only got stronger.

When he realized what he had to do, he almost got sick.

Three years of work down the drain.

It was crazy. Yet…unavoidable.

He went to the phone to call his agent.

GABE WAS BEWILDERED BY Molly's explanation. "Simone didn't have a sister."

"Yes, she did, she just didn't know it. I was eleven years younger."

"That's incredible." Though now that he knew what to look for, he could see the similarities between the two women. *Oh my God*. He'd fallen in love with Simone's sister.

It was too ironic for words.

"Is this why you're so adamant about putting your house up for sale?"

She nodded, then got out of her seat and went to the window.

He watched her. Even though he didn't want to feel anything, the sight of her got to him. Her dress was casual, but also the sexiest thing he'd ever seen her in. She'd done this on purpose, he told himself. Simone had used the same trick, time after time and he'd always fallen for it.

"I wanted to tell you the first time you kissed me, Gabe."

"So why didn't you?"

"I was scared. I *really* like you, you know."

"Your honesty is disarming. And also highly selective."

She winced, then raised her head. "Not really. Usually I'm honest to a fault. That's what anyone would tell you. It's just this one thing that I decided to keep to myself."

"It was a pretty big thing to keep secret."

"Well, yeah, maybe. But think of it from my point of view. I'd never met my sister. If she were alive today, she wouldn't even know me. And if she *had* found out about me, I guarantee you she wouldn't have been happy to meet me."

"Why do you say that?"

"Because I'm the reason her mother left."

He'd wanted to stay cold and detached, but it was simply impossible. He saw Molly's pain and he couldn't help but feel for her. "Tell me what happened, Molly."

"I shouldn't. I promised my mother I wouldn't."

He couldn't hold himself back. He crossed the room to her and put an arm over her shoulder. He thought he could guess part of the story. "Your mother was pregnant with you when she left her family?"

Molly nodded. "When her husband found out about the affair and the pregnancy, he gave her an ultimatum. She could either get an abortion and stay in the marriage. Or she had to leave. Without Simone."

"Oh my God." He couldn't believe this. "He had no right to force her to make that choice."

"No, he didn't. But when my mother tried to defy him, he took Simone and left the country. He came here to Canada with everything, all their belongings, all the money."

"Andrea should have pursued legal action."

"But she was trapped. You see my father didn't know she was married and that she had another child. She was afraid he would leave her if he found out." Molly hesitated. "She's still afraid he would leave her."

It was an incredible story. Gabe didn't know what to make of it. Was it even true? And if it was, did it change anything?

Molly had still lied to him.

"Why did you wait so long to come to Summer Island?" Simone should have been the one to hear this story first. She'd been so marked by her mother's abandonment. She'd deserved to know the truth.

"My mother didn't tell me about this until after Simone was dead. I guess she felt overwhelmed by guilt and had to confess to someone. She went to the memorial service, by the way. The church was full, but she stood outside with the rest of Simone's fans and paid tribute as best she could."

"That's crazy." The whole story was crazy.

"I know. Gabe, I'm so sorry. You probably don't believe me, but if it hadn't been for my mother, I would have told everyone the truth right at the beginning."

He didn't want to see anything from Molly's perspective. Her deception felt huge right now.

And yet a part of him was relieved.

He'd thought she wanted to leave the island because she didn't feel the same way about him as he did about her. But she'd just said that she did care, that she cared a lot.

How much?

And how much did he care about her?

When she started to cry, he felt even more conflicted.

"Sit down, Molly. It's okay."

"It's *not* okay. Nick Lancaster is going to publish a book that will destroy my parents' marriage. And on top of that, you and Jennifer think I'm an impostor."

"Impostor is a little harsh."

"A *little* harsh?" She choked on a sob. "Gabe, all I wanted was to find out what my sister had been like. I didn't want to upset anyone or make any claims on her estate or anything like that. I just wanted to get to know her. Is that so awful?"

She was right, he realized. As Simone's half sister, she *could* have made a claim on Simone's estate. But despite the fact that Molly clearly wasn't a wealthy woman, she hadn't done that.

Didn't that speak to a certain level of integrity? Or was he just so crazy about her that he would grasp at straws to come up with an excuse to forgive her for lying to him?

"Look, Molly, everything you're saying makes sense. It's just that Simone is a hot button with me. Hell, you know the stories."

She seemed to calm down a little at that. "Yes. But in that respect, don't you think it's better that you got to know me first, before you found out I was her sister?"

"You mean you didn't want me to be attracted to you because I knew you were Simone's sister?"

"Something like that." Molly swallowed. "You *did* like me. Right?"

Oh, God. Gabe didn't have a clue how to answer her. Of course he'd liked her. But that was before he'd found out she was Simone's half sister.

Gently he disengaged from her and went over to his desk to pick up his cup of coffee. It was cold, but that didn't matter. He just needed to buy a few moments so he could think.

Simone had been his temptress and in many ways his nemesis, from the first night he'd met her. But though she had teased him, and encouraged him, and led him on time and time again, it wasn't fair for him to blame her for the mess he'd made of his life.

When he'd married Nessa, he should have turned his back on Simone and her charms.

But he hadn't.

Now he'd unwittingly started to fall for her half sister.

The question was, would falling for Molly be as lethal to his happiness as falling for Simone had been?

CHAPTER EIGHTEEN

NICK ASKED JENNIFER IF she would take him hiking that afternoon. She seemed surprised by the request, but she agreed.

"Don't worry about getting home in time to prepare tea," her aunt told her. "Your father and I will take care of that today."

They drove to Arbutus Park and tackled an eight-mile route. It was arduous, with lots of ups and downs, but Nick relished the opportunity for a real workout and Jennifer had no trouble matching his pace.

The trail led them to a lookout point. A million-dollar ocean view worthy of a whole series of postcards. Jennifer stretched out on a rock and gave a satisfied sigh.

"I haven't done this in a long time. Isn't it great up here?"

"Absolutely." He took his camera out of his pack, but instead of snapping shots of the scenery, he focused on Jenn as she lay there with her eyes closed.

He zoomed in for a close-up. Then another. And another. Until Jenn opened one eye. "Hey? What are you doing?"

He put the camera away, then went to lie next to her. "This."

He placed his mouth softly over hers. She made a quiet, happy sound, then turned into him. Why did she feel so good? Taste so good? Nick couldn't think of anything but how badly he wanted her. It didn't take long for their kissing to reach a point of no return.

"Can we do this here?" he asked, his hand on the snap closure to her shorts. "It is a public park, isn't it?"

"We were the only car in the parking lot."

Still, they made a concession to modesty by moving to the cover of some bushes. Making love in the brilliant sunshine was completely different from the previous night. There wasn't an inch of her that he didn't know by the end.

"You are beautiful."

She snuggled her head onto his chest and wrapped her legs around his. "I feel like Eve in the Garden of Eden. If I offer you an apple, you'd better say no."

They dozed until the sun dipped toward the horizon and they were chilled enough to need their clothes. As they dressed, he tried to imagine himself back in New York in a little over a week.

It was hard.

But he had to get back…to his mother and his friends and the apartment that was sure to be full of dust after all this time.

Not to mention his next book. He'd handed in the proposal three months ago and his agent had just given him the green light today. In fact, she'd urged him to start working on it right away.

Poor Michele. He'd shocked her badly. He wasn't sure she was ever going to recover.

He did up his belt, then passed Jennifer her hiking boots. As she loosened the laces to put them on, he thought about all the things that had gone unsaid between them. They'd have to talk soon. Usually he loved uncomplicated, no-strings attached sex, but it wasn't right with Jenn.

She'd need something more, but he wasn't sure what.

"Could you see yourself coming to New York City at all?"

She lifted her head, surprised, then focused back on her boots.

"Winter is your slow season, right? Maybe you could take a vacation…"

Finished with the laces, she got to her feet and brushed debris from her backside. "Nick. Don't do this, okay?"

"What?" He rose slowly to join her.

"Don't give me the we'll always be friends speech. You know as well as I do that we can make all the plans we want. We can promise to e-mail and phone and maybe get together once in a while. But it won't happen."

He tried to put his arms around her, but she backed away.

"Today was great. So was last night. I'm not sorry it happened. Really, I'm not."

"I wasn't going to—"

"Yes, you were." She smiled weakly. "But it's okay. And I'm okay. I think I am going to do some traveling this winter. I was thinking of Australia. Simone and I always wanted to go there one day."

Australia. Without him. "I've always wanted to see Australia, too," he admitted. "But it's a hard place to visit when you don't like to fly."

She broke out into her first honest-to-goodness smile of the day. "You're afraid of flying?"

He shrugged.

"No wonder your poor Rover is in such bad shape."

He ignored the teasing. What he couldn't ignore was the fact that she wasn't trying to talk him into traveling with her.

JENNIFER KEPT UP A BRAVE face for the rest of the evening and for the next few days, too. The last thing she wanted was for Nick to guess that she'd fallen in love with him. It was bad enough that her dad and aunt knew. They were scrambling over themselves to create opportunities for her and Nick to be alone.

By Friday, Jennifer was ready to crack from the pressure. She wanted to savor every minute with Nick, but at the same time it was so hard not to show him how she felt. To live fully in the moment without thinking that tomorrow Nick was going to pack his things in that old Rover of his and drive off forever.

After breakfast, Nick tried to talk her into driving into Cedarbrae with him to return some library books.

"I've got to do a few loads of laundry."

"Okay." His face betrayed clear disappointment. "How about a picnic when I get back?"

"Sure. That would be great." And it

would. She was not going to let her fear about the future spoil this last day with Nick.

An hour later, Jennifer was hanging towels on the line in the backyard when she heard a car drive up. She'd been expecting Nick, but it didn't sound like his Rover.

She added a final peg to the towel she was holding in place, then walked around to the front of the house. She was surprised to see a stylish woman in her mid-forties, dressed in a business suit and super-high heels, step out of a rented sedan.

"Can I help you?" She doubted that she was going to be able to. Her rooms were all full. This woman hadn't booked ahead.

"I hope so." The woman walked around the back of her car with a briefcase in hand. She gave Jennifer the sort of smile that said, *I'm very busy but I'm making an effort to be pleasant,* then pushed at the bridge of her glasses. They were black and looked expensive and made her seem very smart.

"I'm Jennifer March. I'm afraid we're fully booked right now."

"That's okay. My name is Michele Ashburn and I won't need a room. I'm here to see Nick Lancaster."

GABE STARED AT THE SIGNED contract Molly had left on his desk several days ago. He still hadn't called the prospective purchasers to tell them the owner had accepted their offer. Since Molly had told him her secret, he'd been in a state of shock.

But several days had passed and he felt clearheaded at last. He'd phoned her this morning and asked if she could come by one more time. He'd told her he had a counteroffer for her, which was contractually impossible, of course, since the prospective purchaser was the one with the offer on the table.

But this counteroffer didn't come from the prospective purchaser.

His door opened and Flora stuck her head inside. "Weren't you doing an open house for the Whitehalls today?"

"Change of plans." He waved her away.

The Whitehalls wouldn't be happy but he didn't give a damn. He couldn't concentrate on anything, except the view out his window and…

There she was. He spotted her crossing the street from the bakery. He drank in the sight of her, dressed ultra conservatively in slacks and a blazer. She'd have looked businesslike if it wasn't for her head of wild red curls.

He scrambled out of his chair and was waiting when she entered the reception area. "Molly."

"Hi, Gabe."

Flora shot a curious glance at him as he ushered Molly into his office. He made sure to close the door, then waved Molly to a seat.

She looked at him apprehensively. "What's the counteroffer? I told you I wanted to accept their offer."

"I know. The counteroffer is mine." He pulled his chair over so there wouldn't be a desk between them. "I've been thinking about what you told me."

"Yes…?"

"Your sister had my head spinning for many years. It scares me to think that I could lose control of my life like that again."

"My sister didn't know what she wanted. Or who she wanted." Molly's chest rose on a deep breath. "I do."

His heart had been beating rapidly since he'd spotted her. Now it went into overdrive. She was so sexy and fun and honest. At least, he used to think she was honest. Deep down, he still did.

"Gabe, I've booked a flight back to Toronto. I'm planning to leave the island tomorrow. But before I go, I need to say something. I've never told a man this before, so I'm a little nervous, but I've had a crush on you since the first time I met you."

"A *crush?*"

"More than that," she admitted. "I know we haven't been dating long. But I'm crazy about you, Gabe. It might be love. I wish I'd had a chance to find out if it was."

Now this was honesty. How could he hold her deception against her, when she was brave enough to put her entire heart on the line like this?

He couldn't.

He picked up her signed contract. "You know what I want to do with this?"

She watched as he tore it in two, then tossed it into the trash.

"I have a different offer for you, Molly. I hope you'll think it's a better one. How about you stay on Summer Island? Because I'm crazy about you, too, and I couldn't stand it if you left."

"NICK'S IN TOWN RIGHT NOW, but I'm expecting him back soon."

From the woman's accent, Jennifer assumed she was a New Yorker, like Nick. Michele Ashburn must have been pretty desperate to see him if she'd traveled all this way.

"Would you like to wait for him on the porch?" Jennifer offered. "I'd be happy to get you something to drink."

"Actually, would it be possible for you and I to talk first?"

That was strange. Jennifer shrugged. "I can make the time. Just give me a moment and I'll bring out some lemonade." She gestured to the cushioned chairs. "Take a seat and make yourself at home."

As Jennifer arranged glasses on a tray in the kitchen, she thought how disappointed her dad and aunt were going to be to have missed this latest, intriguing visitor. They wouldn't be back from their overnight trip to Victoria until noon the next day. She poured lemonade, added ice cubes, then went back outside.

"Did you just come from New York?" Jennifer handed Michele a glass, then sat in the chair next to hers.

"Yes. It was quite a journey. Flying to Seattle was fairly straightforward, but then I had to take about twenty-nine ferries to get here."

Jennifer laughed. "Yes. We are remote. That's the way we like it, too."

"Must be hell on the FedEx delivery-man."

They were making polite chitchat. Jennifer wondered why this woman had asked to talk to her. Surely she wasn't simply curious about life in the slow lane?

"You haven't figured out who I am. Or why I'm here. I can see you're trying to." Michele tipped her head and regarded Jennifer closely. "He hasn't told you about me?"

"What should Nick have told me?" she asked, trying to sound only mildly interested.

"Well, first let me explain that I'm his literary agent."

Now Jennifer remembered hearing her voice before. "You booked his reservation."

"That's right. Though I might have picked a different place if I'd been able to predict the future."

"Pardon?"

"Clearly, Nick decided to renege on his book deal because of you."

"He's reneging on his book deal?"

Michele looked at her like she was an annoying child. "You must know this. He had his bank transfer the advance to my office yesterday. He told me to get him out of the contract. He won't deliver the manuscript."

Jennifer stared at the woman, stunned. This couldn't be true.

And yet literary agents didn't travel across continents on whims. No wonder Michele was looking rather grim right now. She earned her money based on commissions. Which meant that if Nick was giving back his money, she'd have to give back hers, too.

"Nick can't back out on this book," Jennifer said. "It means too much to him."

Again, Michele looked surprised. "Is that really the way you feel?"

"Yes."

"Then why—" Michele was diverted by the sound of an approaching vehicle. "Isn't that Nick's Rover?"

Thank heavens. He had a lot of explaining to do. But clearly Michele intended to speak to him first. She was out of her chair and halfway across the driveway before Jennifer had time to move. She decided to give them a moment and took the tray of drinks back inside. By the time she'd returned, Michele and Nick were talking. Michele hadn't even given him time to get out of the vehicle.

"But I don't understand. She says she wants you to publish the book."

"Let me get out of here, okay, Michele?"

His agent backed off, and Nick hopped to the ground. He closed the door to the Rover, then headed for the porch. Though he didn't touch her, the intimacy of his gaze made Jennifer feel as if he had.

"You've met Michele?"

She nodded, holding back the questions she was dying to ask. What was going on here? Why had he returned his advance? Was he really not going to produce the book? And most important of all why was he doing this?

Nick sighed, then turned to face his agent. "I can't believe you traveled all this way."

"You're talking about a lot of money, Nick."

"And *you're* talking about a lot of miles. You could have phoned."

"Gee, Nick. I thought you'd be happier to see me." Michele made the effort to smile. "Come on. Let's sit down and talk."

As Nick settled on one of the chairs, Jennifer hung back. "I've got stuff I should be doing. Why don't you guys catch up. I'll be in the kitchen if you need me."

Nick rose as if to stop her, but Michele put a hand to his arm. "Wait, Nick. I think it is a good idea if we chat alone first."

NICK WAS VERY UNCOMFORTABLE with the idea that Michele had traveled so far to talk to him about this. "I wish you had called first, Michele."

"This is too important for a phone conversation. By the way, I had a chance to chat with Jennifer. She didn't even know that you'd decided to withdraw your book."

"I didn't tell her because she'd only try to talk me out of it."

"Maybe you should let her do exactly that."

"If I did, I know she'd regret her decision later. Jennifer was against this book from the start. She and Simone were very good friends. They had secrets that Jennifer would prefer no one find out about."

"So cut those bits out," Michele suggested.

"That would take away the heart of the book." Nick shook his head. "There's no point in arguing. I've made up my mind. That's why I wish you'd let me know before you came all this way. I could have saved you a lot of time."

He was about to add and money, until he recalled that money was exactly why Michele had come. If she could talk him into publishing the book, she'd make a lot more than a return plane fare would have set her back.

Michele crossed her arms over her chest. "You're going to lose your credibility with the publishing company if you don't produce what they're expecting."

"Initially, maybe. But the next contract is already in the bag. As long as that book sells well, I think they'll get over the loss of revenue from this one."

"Nick. You disappoint me. Think of the time lag between books. The inevitable dip in your royalty figures."

And *hers* as well. He didn't blame Michele for seeing everything in terms of the bottom line. That was her job and why he'd hired her.

"I'm sorry, Michele."

She looked away, bitter disappointment making her look older and harder than her forty-plus years. "You really must love her."

"Yeah. **I do.**"

Now where had that come from? Nick didn't have to think too long to figure it out. *Idiot.* Of course he loved her. He'd been a fool to deny it for as long as he had.

JENNIFER MIXED BERRIES AND white choco-
late chunks into her scones, then checked
the time. Only thirty minutes had passed
since she'd left Nick and Michele on the
porch, but it felt like an hour.

"Hey, Jenn."

She whirled around at the sound of his
voice. He looked tired, but strangely
happy, too. His talk with Michele must
have gone well.

Jenn sunk her fists into the dough as he
sat at one of the stools and faced her over
the island.

"What's going on?" she asked him.
"Your agent told me that you'd pulled the
book."

He nodded.

"Did you tell her you changed your
mind?" No reaction. "Please tell me you
changed your mind." Still no reaction.

"Nick, answer me, please. What's going
on with your book?"

"I'm not going to publish it."

"But why?" Had he done this crazy

thing for her? And why had he started to smile at her that way? As if he was the one with a secret for a change.

"Nick, I meant what I told you the other day. I support your book. I really do."

"That's what you say now. But you're still mad at Simone. What about when that fades—and it will. You're not the type to stay angry forever. I don't want this book to be something that ever stands between us."

He said that as if there was an us. As if they had a future. Oh, she so wanted to believe that there was and there could be. But first she had to set things straight.

"You're right that I'm not one to hold a grudge. I'm already past being angry at Simone. I think I've even forgiven Molly."

She picked bits of dough off her hands, then grabbed the apple box from under the counter.

"Here. Use whatever you want."

"But—"

"I'm serious. No strings attached." She wanted him to be clear that she wasn't trying to buy any sort of commitment out of him. "Even if I never see you again after tomorrow, I still want you to use whatever photographs you need for the book. And you can have your pick from my album, too."

Nick stood and rounded the island. He put his hands on her hips and looked into her eyes intently. "You're sure about this?"

She caught her breath. Pressed her lips together to keep from thinking about how badly she wanted to kiss him. Lord, but she loved this man. "Yes. I'm sure."

And then, as if he'd read her mind, he kissed her. Forgetting about her sticky hands, she cupped his head to pull him closer. He leaned her into the counter and pressed his body tightly to hers.

"Michele," she suddenly remembered. "Where is she?"

Nick drew back a few inches. "Rushing to catch the afternoon ferry to the mainland. In a little while I'll call her and make her a very happy woman."

Remembering how grim Michele had

looked when she arrived, Jennifer suggested, "Maybe you should call her right now."

He groaned, as she ran her hands down his back. "I have other ideas for the next thirty minutes. Didn't your dad and aunt say they were going to be gone until tomorrow?" He touched the top button of her blouse suggestively.

"We have other guests," she reminded him.

"Right. So making out on the kitchen counter isn't an option?"

"Well…not right now." She felt so giddy she could hardly think straight. There was something different about Nick. Ever since he'd come in from his talk with Michele he'd had this funny light in his eyes.

"Will you marry me?"

She pulled away from him, stunned. "Did I hear that right?"

"I love you, Jenn."

Had he really said that? Yes. That look on his face was happiness. And she'd bet the same look was mirrored on her face right now.

"Jenn? You're leaving me hanging here."

As if there could be any doubt. "I love you, too. But Nick…I'm tied to this island and the B and B and my family."

He smoothed the hair on the side of her face. "You think I don't know that? I've been doing some quick thinking here. The bed-and-breakfast business is slow November through February, right?"

"Yes."

"So in the winter months we'll live in New York City."

She closed her eyes, imagining how exciting that would be. His offer was so, so tempting. And yet, still impossible. "I can't leave Dad and Annie alone for that long."

"Of course not. I'll have to get a bigger place in New York. Maybe we could get two apartments on the same floor."

"You mean Dad and Annie will come with us?"

"Naturally. They're family, right?"

"Oh, Nick. And in the spring and summer we'll come back here?"

"It's a great place for me to write." He kissed her again. "Oh, one more thing. It's about my book."

She narrowed her eyes. He wasn't going to change his mind again, was he?

"I'm dedicating it to you."

EPILOGUE

Book launch on Summer Island, one year later

"So now the entire world knows all our secrets." Harrison touched his glass of champagne to Jennifer's.

Then to Aidan's. And Gabe's.

The four of them had slipped out to the B and B's porch after Nick finished his reading. He was now being inundated with requests to sign copies of his book.

Jennifer was so proud of him. He handled all the attention and praise so graciously, with his typical offhand charm.

And the praise had been pretty lavish so far. Great reviews from the places that mattered. And though it had been available for only a week, his book was already creeping onto some of the bestseller lists.

"Yeah, Nick didn't miss a trick, did he?" Gabe took a sip of the champagne. "I still can't believe you're the one who wrote that song, Jenn."

"Simone milked it to the max, didn't she?" Aidan said. "Had everyone wondering who the special forget-me-not friend was. And Jenn just played along."

"After a while I think I forgot she didn't write the lyrics. She sang it so often, the song just became synonymous with Simone."

That was one negative that came with the publication of Nick's book. She'd been inundated by journalists and talk show hosts who wanted to hear *her* story.

How did it feel to have your lyrics become the number one song in America? Were you angry that Simone never gave you credit for your contribution? Are you going to sue for your share of the profits?

"I feel really terrible about the situation," Harrison said. "I still wish you'd let me settle some of the revenue from Simone's estate with you, Jenn."

"I definitely don't want that. Just buy lots of copies of Nick's books." She bumped her hip teasingly against Harrison. "I'll get my royalty payments that way."

He retaliated by tapping her shoulder with his fist. "Gladly. Nick is good. Damned good. But the best thing about this book is that Nick got us talking to one another again."

It was true. And they were doing more than talking. Gabe and Harrison had started sailing together again. Jennifer had never thought she'd see the day.

"The biggest surprise had to be when Andrea DeRosier—I mean Springfield— showed up," Aidan said.

Everyone nodded and fell silent. Simone's mother had arrived for the book launch with Molly and they were still inside with the crowd. Molly had promised to introduce them all later. Harrison was particularly anxious to meet the woman who once would have been his mother-in-law. And of course she would always be Autumn's grandmother.

It was great to have Simone's mother finally on Summer Island. But Molly had been right to fear exposure of her mother's secret. When her father found out that Andrea had deserted a husband and daughter to be with him, he'd divorced her and still wouldn't speak to her.

The front door opened and Molly and Nick stepped outside. Molly went straight to Gabe while Nick headed for Jennifer. She reached for his arm and pulled it around her waist.

"How's your mom doing, Molly?" Jennifer asked.

"Better. In a way, I think the divorce was a relief for her. She had so much guilt…now it's out in the open and she can start to deal with it. And it's been good for her healing process to come to Summer Island."

"Call her out here," Harrison said. "Justine and I would like to invite her for dinner. It's time she met her granddaughter."

Molly's eyes filled with tears. "She'd love that. And it would be great for everyone to become better acquainted before our wedding." She smiled at Gabe, who responded by wrapping an arm around her shoulders. "But right now Mom is talking to Jenn's father. I believe they're quite taken with each other."

"Oh?" Jennifer wondered just what Molly meant by taken.

Molly laughed. "Wouldn't that be crazy?"

"Yeah. It sure would." But sometimes the most unlikely couples made for the best marriages. Jennifer looked up at her husband, still in partial disbelief that he really was hers. A year ago, that outcome had seemed utterly impossible to her.

"So what's next for the famous author?" Aidan asked.

Nick tightened his hold on Jenn. "If you ask my wife, it would be a travel book on Australia."

"But I have to get him on the plane first. Nick doesn't like to travel anywhere he can't reach in his trusty old Land Rover."

"Hey, it got me to you, didn't it?"

She couldn't argue with that. And why should she care about seeing faraway places anyway, when she had Nick and her friends right here?

Rae and Justine slipped out the front door next. "Hey, no fair drinking all the champagne without us," Rae protested.

Harrison stepped up to fill two more flutes from the magnum on the table. "Better?"

"Much," Justine said. "Look at this. We've got the entire forget-me-not gang together. What should we drink to?"

Could there be any doubt? Jennifer raised her glass to all her friends. Justine and Harrison. Aidan and Rae. Molly and Gabe. And her own wonderful Nick. "To the success of Nick's book. And to Simone, the reason we're all here today."

Forget me not, my one true friend.

Jennifer knew none of them ever would.

* * * * *

My husband could see beauty in a mud puddle. Literally. "Look at that, Louise," he'd say after a heavy spring rain. "Have you ever seen so many amazing colors in mud?"

I'd look and see nothing except brown, but he'd pick up a stick and swirl the mud till the colors of the earth emerged, and all of a sudden I'd see the world through his eyes—extraordinary instead of mundane.

Roy was my mirror to life. Four years ago when he died, it cracked wide open, and I've been living a smashed-up, sleepwalking life ever since.

If he were here on this balmy August night I'd be sailing with him instead of baking cheese straws in preparation for Tuesday-night quilting club with Patsy. I'd be striving for sex appeal in Bermuda shorts and bare-toed sandals instead of opting for comfort in walking shoes and a twill skirt with enough elastic around the waist to make allowances for two helpings of lemon-cream pie.

Not that I mind Patsy. Just the opposite. I love her. She's the only person besides Roy who creates wonder wherever she goes. (She creates mayhem, too, but we won't get into that.) She's my mirror now, as well as my compass.

Of course, I have my daughter, Diana, but I refuse to be the kind of mother who defines herself through her children. Besides, she has her own life now, a husband and a baby on the way.

I slide the last cheese straws into the oven and then go into my office and open e-mail.

From: "Miss Sass" <patsyleslie@hotmail.com>
To: "The Lady" <louisejernigan@yahoo.com>
Sent: Tuesday, August 15, 6:00 PM
Subject: Dangerous Tonight

Hey, Lady,

I'm feeling dangerous tonight. Hot to trot, if you know what I mean. Or can you even remember?☺ Look out, bridge club, here I come. I'm liable to end up dancing on the tables instead of bidding three spades. Whose turn is it to drive, anyhow? Mine or thine?

XOXOX

Patsy

P.S. Lord, how did we end up in a club with no men?

This e-mail is typical "Patsy." She's the only person I know who makes me laugh all the time. I guess that's why I e-mail her about ten times a day. She lives right next door, but e-mail satisfies my urge to be instantly and constantly in touch with her without having to interrupt the flow of my life. Sometimes we even save the good stuff for e-mail.

From: "The Lady" <louisejernigan@yahoo.com>
To: "Miss Sass" <patsyleslie@hotmail.com>

Sent: Tuesday, August 15, 6:10 PM
Subject: Re: Dangerous Tonight
So, what else is new, Miss Sass? You're always dangerous. If you had a weapon, you'd be lethal.☺
Hugs,
Louise
P.S. What's this about men? I thought you said your libido was dead?

I press Send then wait. Her reply is almost instantaneous.

From: "Miss Sass" <patsyleslie@hotmail.com>
To: "The Lady" <louisejernigan@yahoo.com>
Sent: Tuesday, August 15, 6:12 PM
Subject: Re: Dangerous Tonight
Ha! If I had a *brain* I'd be lethal.
And I said my libido was in hibernation, not DEAD!
Jeez, Louise!!!!!
P

Patsy loves to have the last word, so I shut off my computer.

* * * * *

*Want to find out what happens
to their friendship
when Patsy and Louise both find the
perfect man?*

*Don't miss
CONFESSIONS OF A NOT-SO-DEAD LIBIDO
by Peggy Webb,
coming to Harlequin NEXT
in November 2006.*

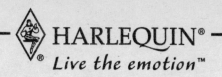

Harlequin® Historical
Historical Romantic Adventure!

Imagine a time of chivalrous knights and unconventional ladies, roguish rakes and impetuous heiresses, rugged cowboys and spirited frontierswomen— these rich and vivid tales will capture your imagination!

Harlequin Historical . . . they're too good to miss!

HHDIR06

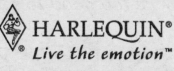

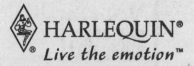

SPECIAL EDITION™

Emotional, compelling stories that capture the intensity of
living, loving and creating a family in today's world.

Silhouette
Desire

Modern, passionate reads that are powerful and provocative.

Romances that are sparked by danger and fueled by passion.

From today to forever, these love stories offer
today's woman fairytale romance.

Action-filled romances with strong, sexy, savvy women who save the day.

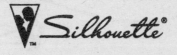